G
MOTHMAN

BY

Jay Noel

Emma,
Beware
the Mothman!

Jay Noel

Quixotic
Publishing

Gateway Mothman
Copyright © 2018 by Jay Noel
All rights reserved.

Gateway Mothman is a work of fiction. The characters, incidents, and dialogues are products of the author's imagination and are not to be construed as real. Any resemblance to actual events or persons, living or dead, is entirely coincidental.

In accordance with the U.S. Copyright Act of 1976, no part of this publication may be reproduced, distributed, or transmitted in any form or by any means. The scanning, uploading, and electronic sharing of any part of this book without the permission of the publisher is unlawful piracy and theft of the author's intellectual property. If you would like to use material from this book (other than for review purposes), prior written permission must be obtained by contacting the publisher. Thank you for your support of the author's rights.

Quixotic Publishing LLC
Royal Palm Beach, FL
www.quixoticpublishing.com

Edited by: Alex Neupert (Adelysium Editorial Services)
Cover by: Dominic Reyes

Gateway Mothman / Jay Noel. — First Edition

ISBN 978-1-939588-23-4 (Print Edition)
ISBN 978-1-939588-24-1 (Ebook Edition)

The Dark Projects Books:

By Miranda Hardy and Jay Noel

<u>Black-Eyed Kids</u>
Death Knocks
Marcus
Death Returns

By Jay Noel

<u>Mothman</u>
Gateway Mothman

*For all the people fighting the good fight,
especially those involved with
Just Moms STL and Coldwater Creek – Just the Facts
Please.*

They cannot ignore us any longer.

"Average people and the average community can change the world. You can do it just based on common sense, determination, persistence and patience."
~ Lois Gibbs, American Environmental Activist

PROLOGUE

IT WAS THE day before my senior year when I first saw the Mothman, but the events leading up to it started long before that. Personally, what set everything in motion was the day my twin brother died when we were nine years old, but many would say the beginning of the end started when our brightest scientists started playing with uranium.

Last year, we read about the Manhattan Project in U.S. History class. Mr. Klaas simply glossed over that part and got into the heart of World War II in the Pacific and spent most of our time talking about the bombing of Hiroshima and Nagasaki. The atom bomb. But before Big Boy and Fat Man were dropped over Japan to end the war, there was the Manhattan Project.

Growing up in the northwestern part of St. Louis, at least twenty-five percent of the kids going to my school had a parent who worked for the Matzenbach

Corporation in some capacity. One of its divisions worked with the U.S. government and had dumped a bunch of radioactive crap in my backyard back in the 1940s.

OK, so the poison wasn't in my backyard exactly, but it was pretty damn close. Over the years, not much of a fuss was made about the radioactive landfill, but all it took was a simple thing like a horrendous stench to finally wake us up from our apathy. Freshman year, you couldn't go outside without gagging from the stink. It was truly horrible. My neighbors finally started complaining, and people got more organized about getting the EPA's attention. Meetings were held every week. Neither of my parents attended those meetings, but everyone kept us updated about the lack of progress.

Bridgetowne had suffered from a devastating tornado just a few years prior that had wiped out a bunch of houses near us. Even though most of the homes and buildings had been rebuilt or repaired, the town was still reeling from the trauma. The last thing we needed was another natural disaster. All the signs that something awful was going to happen were all around us, but we ignored them.

I had spent that summer hanging out with my friends and working part time. Meanwhile, St. Louis had been a ticking time bomb, and none of us knew it. Up until then, we only dealt with what was directly in front of us. With St. Louis on the verge of catastrophe, the Mothman descended upon the Gateway City.

CHAPTER 1

YET ANOTHER SUPERHERO movie, yet another disappointment. Maybe having such high expectations kept me from enjoying these disasters. Shannon kept defending the film, saying that I was being a geek-snob. Of course, she would say that, since she never read the actual comic books. Dylan and Brandon were on her side, but I was sticking to my guns.

"But Jonah, if you make the movie too much like the comic books, you're going to turn off the typical moviegoer," Shannon said as she got in my car.

I slid behind the steering wheel. It was August, but it felt like October. Inside my car, it was more like November. "I totally get it. They have to make the money, but they don't have to utterly destroy the story lines and make all the superheroes look like idiots in the process."

"I dunno. I think it was literally kick-ass," Brandon said as he and Dylan took the back seat. "I read the comic books, but I don't see a problem with the movie."

Dylan easily stood six-foot-five, and he let out a grunt when he scrunched his lanky body and settled into the seat. "Special effects kicked ass."

"It's always about the special effects with you," I said without turning around to look at him. "I'm talking about the story. What they did was sacrilegious."

Shannon fiddled with her ponytail and gave me a sideways grin. "I'm too hungry to argue. I'm starving. Let's get some pizza or something."

"You're just pissed because I'm right and you're wrong." I started the car and turned on the headlights. "How about the Chinese buffet?"

"Dude, no!" Brandon slapped the back of my headrest. "Damn, Jonah. Why do you love going to that place? They serve dog meat there."

I put the car in drive and pulled out slowly before joining the long line of cars trying to get out of the parking lot. "They do not. That's such a myth. Besides, I thought there wasn't a buffet you didn't love."

Brandon didn't appreciate the fat joke and flipped me off. "The last time I ate there, I literally got the runs."

Dylan gave Brandon a quick jab to the shoulder. "You got sick from the soft serve ice cream. They probably don't clean the machine out. You had four or five bowls of that crap."

"Of course." Shannon crossed her thin arms. "I say pizza and you want Chinese food."

"You're biased since you're Chinese," Brandon said with a chuckle.

I slammed on the brakes hard enough to nearly give everyone whiplash. "Take that back, dumbass."

Brandon rubbed his neck. "Oh, so sorry. Vietnamese."

My friends all knew my biggest pet peeve. I hated how people lumped all Asians together, and Brandon knew I hated being called Chinese. He must not have been too ticked off, because he didn't call me a Chink.

Shannon stopped pretending to be mad and turned on the radio. "Actually, Chinese sounds good. I've got a hankering for some crab rangoonies."

"Hell yeah." I turned onto Rock Road and started for the Chinese buffet. "I don't know who General Tso is, but he makes some mighty fine chicken."

"Now I'm hungry," Dylan chimed in.

"I have to watch my sodium intake," Brandon said in almost a whisper. "I might have to get an actual blood test the next time I see my doctor."

I was afraid of needles too, but Brandon was afraid of everything. "It's just a quick prick on your finger. No big deal."

"No, they'll literally have to stab my arm with a big

needle and get a bunch of tubes this time." Brandon leaned back and covered his face. "Maybe it'll just be vegetables and a little rice for me."

"It's a buffet, man," I said in an effort to make him feel better. "You can have anything you want. And I'm pretty sure the soft serve ice cream is low in sodium, if you don't mind getting the Hershey-squirts again." The entire car cried out in disgust, but I couldn't help but laugh. Hersey-squirts was one of my all-time favorite vulgar phrases.

The Rock Road was a main road that cut through Bridgetowne, but the traffic that night was thin. It had to be only nine o'clock. For a Saturday night before the beginning of the new school year, things were pretty dead.

"Can you turn on the heater, just on my feet?" Shannon asked.

I shook my head. "It's freaking August. I'm not turning on the heater."

"But it's cold!" Shannon reached out to the controls. "Just for a second."

I was about to say something about her always being cold when a feeling of dread came over me. For the last nine years, I had become very acquainted with what a panic attack felt like. I had them all the time. But this was different. Everyone in the car had become totally silent, and the fearful look in Shannon's eyes mirrored what I was feeling.

From my rearview mirror, Dylan and Brandon looked straight ahead with their mouths drawn slightly open. The song on the radio faded until nothing but static came out of the speakers. Shannon switched channels, only to find more static.

"What the hell is going on?" Brandon asked nobody in particular.

On the other side of the Rock Road, a rusted blue, beat-up old truck drove past us. The driver was an old guy, and he glanced at me with such a weird look on his face, that I let out a gasp. He looked like a living skeleton with big eyes that bulged out of their sockets. His skin was like thin leather pulled tightly over his bony skull. We made eye contact for just a split second, but the smirk he flashed me gave me the chills, as if he knew some dirty secrets I was hiding.

"Is your radio broken?" Shannon asked me.

"It shouldn't be. It was working just fine a second ago," I replied.

Dylan leaned his long body towards us in the front. "Do you feel that?"

"Feel what?" I asked.

"I can't explain it," he answered.

Brandon pulled out his phone but didn't turn it on. "I feel like something really bad is going to happen."

I slowed the car down to thirty, and the jalopy truck continued down the Rock Road until it turned off and disappeared. At that moment, it felt like we were the only car on the street. In the city. In the entire world. The old mall that was being rehabbed was on our right, and the school administration building stood on our left. Even the streetlights seemed to dim, going from their usually bright white to a dull orange.

Something out of the corner of my eye caught my attention, and Shannon must have seen it too. She pressed her face against the side window, her breaths coming out so heavy, she fogged it up. At first, I thought an airplane was crashing towards us from overhead.

"What...what did you see?" Brandon asked.

I pulled over and tried my best to look out the front windshield. "I saw it too."

"Was it a UFO?" Dylan asked. "I've always wanted to see one!"

I opened my side window and stuck my head out. The sky was absolutely clear, and the stars were out in full-force tonight. "I saw something too. It was flying, and it's most definitely unidentified. I guess, yeah, it's a UFO."

Dylan unlocked his door. "Cool, let's get out and see."

I put the car back in park but kept the engine running. Brandon stayed in the car as the rest of us stepped out onto the sidewalk and searched the night sky for whatever dark object had flown right above us a second ago.

"It couldn't have been a plane," Shannon said as she kept her gaze skyward. "Their engines make sounds. Whatever it was, it made no sound at all."

Dylan shook his head. "Man, did I miss it? What did it look like?"

I started to feel dizzy from staring up at the sky for so long, so I closed my eyes. "Honestly, the damn thing had wings."

"That's exactly what I saw!" Shannon grabbed my arm. "Like a giant bird."

"A bird?" Dylan shrugged his shoulders. "Seriously? I'm getting back in the car. It's too cold out here to be birdwatching."

I knew what I had seen, and I continued to watch the sky for it. "It was no ordinary bird. It was huge."

"Whatever." Dylan opened the door, but Brandon got out and joined us.

Brandon had his phone on, and he kept glancing up at the sky and then back down to his phone. "It was probably a vulture or something. They can get pretty big."

Shannon stopped craning her neck. "That makes sense."

It might have been a vulture, but there was no ignoring that heavy feeling of dread that wouldn't let go of me. "Am I the only one having a weird panic attack?"

Brandon put his phone away. "No."

"No." Shannon's eyes grew large, and she looked like she wanted to get back in the car. "And where is everybody? Ever since the mall shut down, this stretch of the road gets pretty quiet, but it's Saturday night."

I got out my phone and checked the time. "Yeah, and it's not that late." I did my best to relax. "The Chinese buffet is only open for another twenty minutes, so we'd better hurry."

Shannon had only taken one step towards my car when the giant bird emerged from the darkness and swooped towards the mall. It was so dark, and the animal was so far away, it was impossible to discern any details. It had wings, but they didn't flap. It reminded me of how hawks flew, just gliding in the air.

"There it is!" Brandon got out his phone to snap a picture, but I knew he wouldn't be able to take a clear one.

Dylan kept his hand on the open door. "Holy crap, that is a huge-ass bird!"

I shut my eyes before opening them again. "Can vultures get that big?"

We watched it fly away in the direction of my subdivision. Some of my neighbors owned guns, and if they saw that thing flying around, they'd shoot it and hang it up on their wall.

"It's not a vulture," Shannon whispered.

Brandon frowned from the low-quality pictures he

had just taken on his phone. "What makes you so sure?"

Shannon gave me the most serious look. It terrified me. "Vultures don't have hands and feet."

We hardly said a word during dinner. As if seeing the weird flying creature just minutes ago wasn't enough, another chain of mysterious things happened immediately after.

Once we got in the car and I started driving, Shannon gave the radio another try. Sure enough, it was working just fine. She found a news station on the AM band, hoping to hear about witnesses who had seen the giant flying monster, but the biggest news story was about how the Cardinals were on a six-game winning streak.

Strangely, the street lights grew brighter as we neared the Chinese buffet. Two or three cars joined us on the Rock Road, and after several more minutes of driving, traffic seemed to pick up a bit. Everything was back to normal.

The Chinese woman up front had greeted us with a smile, but I could tell that she was annoyed that a bunch of us kids had come in fifteen minutes before closing. We weren't the only ones in there, though. It was quiet inside, and the silence lingered in the dining area like a bad stink. We had taken a seat as far away from the windows as possible. Dylan's appetite seemed the only thing unaffected by the night's events. Brandon's fingers still trembled as he picked at his grilled veggies and steamed rice.

I decided to speak up first. "So, what should we do?"

"What did you have in mind?" Shannon asked. "Go to the cops or something?"

Brandon took out his phone and found the police scanner and EMS app. He turned down the volume and placed it against his ear. We all watched him do this for a few minutes, but by the look on his face, there was nothing about the flying creature being reported.

"There's some naked, drunk guy walking near the school," Brandon said with a half-smile.

"Nothing on the radio, nothing on the police scanner." I took another bite of my General Tso's chicken. Even the good general's recipe wasn't making me feel any better. "Maybe when I get home, I'll start checking some of the paranormal message boards. I'll start with the UFO Network and see if people reported seeing something in the area."

Shannon looked lost in her own thoughts. "Good idea."

Dylan put down his fork and leaned over as if he was going to share a secret. "Shannon, are you sure you saw what you think you saw? We didn't get that good of a look at it. It had wings, that's for sure."

"I have 20/10 vision, remember?" Shannon stared at her half-eaten crab rangoon.

I took another swig of my soda and almost laughed out loud. The four of us had been friends since kindergarten, and I jokingly called us a league of superheroes. Each of us had a unique special power that made us a little different from most people.

Dylan, other than being as tall as Godzilla, was a super math genius. He was guaranteed a full ride to Rolla for engineering. Brandon had a photographic memory. Everything he saw or read was stuck in his brain forever. Shannon had super-vision; we started calling her "Eagle Eyes" in middle school. I had hyperthymesia. I could remember, with great detail, nearly every single day of my life going back to when I was nine years old.

Coincidentally, that was when Elijah had died.

The four of us sat there in shock and confusion, and our "super powers" were of no help to us.

"It's our last night of summer break," Shannon said. "This wasn't how I imagined it would end."

I felt exactly the same way. This was not how I wanted to remember the best summer of my life. "What we saw could be anything, really." I looked Shannon straight in the eyes. "It was so dark, even with your sharp vision, the play of the light could have played tricks on you, right?"

Shannon looked like she might argue, but she picked at her food instead. "It's possible."

Dylan finished his third plate, and he looked over at what remained of the buffet as if he was going back for more. "All I can say is, that had to be the weirdest thing to ever happen to me. I'm just glad I had witnesses. No one would believe me."

"Maybe I'll talk to my dad about it," Brandon said.

Brandon's father worked for the big aerospace defense contractor in town, so that made sense. But he was an engineer, a no-nonsense kind of guy. He'd probably laugh at Brandon's story.

"Are you sure that's a good idea?" Shannon asked, as if she was reading my mind like usual.

Brandon replied, "He's not supposed to talk about some of the top-secret aircraft they're building at Aerocorp, but I'll ask if one of their newest planes was flying around here tonight. He'd tell me if there was."

Neither of my parents had such a fascinating job, but they were pretty easy to talk to, as far as parents went. Dad was just a financial chief at a small company, and Mom sold real estate. But if they had heard something from the neighbors talking about a flying…whatever…they'd tell me.

"I'm pretty sure it wasn't an airplane," Shannon said.

"I've read online about super-high-tech aircraft with anti-grav engines that literally make no sound."

Brandon's voice climbed an octave higher, which meant he was getting worked up again. "Jonah's right, what we saw could be anything. We have to keep an open mind."

Dylan stood up and started for the buffet. "I'm not telling anybody. No way."

I turned to Shannon, and she shrugged.

"My mom's too busy to listen anyway," she said.

Brandon and Shannon stared at me, waiting for my declaration.

"I'll casually bring it up with my folks tomorrow morning," I finally said. "My mom is especially good at picking up the local gossip."

Shannon absentmindedly turned on her phone to check for texts. That made no sense since everyone who might have texted her was sitting at our table. "I'm all for keeping an open mind, but I know what I saw." She put her phone down and looked as if she wanted to smack Brandon in the face. "What I saw looked like a man. With wings."

CHAPTER 2

THE NEXT MORNING, I walked past my mom's home office. Since she was a real estate agent, she often spent a lot of time working from the spare bedroom. I couldn't help but stop next to the open doorway and peek inside. Family pictures and a few sales awards hung on the white walls. A wooden desk and chair with a matching bookcase were the only pieces of furniture inside.

I often imagined what it would be like if Elijah had still been alive. I assumed he would have taken the office room eventually. Up until the day he died, we shared a bedroom. With the start of senior year only a day away, it also meant that our eighteenth birthday was coming up.

That time of year had always been tough for me, and my panic attacks usually increased in frequency until after our birthday passed. My counselor believed guilt triggered all my dark thoughts. She was right. Despite acknowledging that I often found myself in a time loop, reliving the day Elijah died over and over again with such detail, I powered through it without the help of any anti-depressant meds.

I walked down the hallway, which was covered in more family photos. As usual, I glanced at the one with all four of us. Mom, Dad, me, and Elijah. We were six years old then, absolute clones of one another. The only way to tell us apart was our eye color. Elijah's eyes were a darker shade of brown, almost black.

Dad was Irish, so he had the fair skin and blue eyes. Mom had moved to the States with her immediate family from Vietnam back in 1978 when she was fifteen years old. According to my dad's side, we looked very ethnic. And to my mom's family, we also looked very ethnic. It was funny, though, when people would stare at me and try to figure out what I was. Chinese? Hawaiian? Japanese?

I took one final look at the picture, staring at Elijah's darker eyes before stepping into the kitchen. The smell of french toast made my stomach rumble. Sunday was Dad's day to take command of the kitchen. Mom usually had work, although she didn't look dressed to run an open house today.

"Good morning," Mom said from the table. She leafed through the newspaper. "I was asleep when you got home last night. How was the movie?"

I sat down with her and started to sift through the advertisements. "Not so great. But then again, Shannon thinks it's all my fault. Superhero movies tend to shun actual comic book readers."

Dad left his cooking and swiveled around to face me. "I've always thought that books were much better than the movie versions."

I nodded and poured myself some orange juice. "No open houses today, Mom?"

"Tomorrow's the first day of school." She put her newspaper down and turned on her iPad. "Along with all the other crazy procrastinators, I thought we could get some school supplies. Did you need any clothes, Elijah?"

Dad and I exchanged bewildered looks. Although Mom called me by my brother's name once in a while, the frequency of her mix-ups always increased as our birthday neared, which was only a week away. I usually ignored the mistake.

"I bet a lot of your wardrobe doesn't fit anymore," Dad said.

I had hit a huge growth spurt my junior year. I went from five-foot-five to nearly six feet in the span of ten months. Dad was only five-eleven, and Mom was barely five feet tall. Mom said kids in America were bigger because of the hormones in the milk and beef.

"Maybe not until winter," I replied. "It doesn't get cold until October, so I think I'm good for another month and a half."

The three of us got quiet, lost in our own little worlds. Mom flipped through her real estate website listings. Dad remained preoccupied with cooking. I stared at the both of them, wondering how to bring up what happened last night. I decided to just throw it out there.

"After the movie, on the way to the Chinese buffet, we saw something really weird in the sky."

Mom's already sharp eyes sharpened even more in disapproval. "You ate Chinese buffet so late? That's so bad for you. All that garbage just sat in your belly overnight."

I couldn't help but laugh. "It's okay, Mom. I skipped lunch yesterday, so I was really hungry. I didn't go crazy with the General Tso's."

"What was weird?" Dad asked, ignoring Mom's concern over my dietary choices.

"We were driving down the Rock Road, and we thought at first that a plane was about to crash. When we got outside, it looked like a giant bird. Really huge. Big enough to snatch a small kid like in that YouTube video."

Mom was still stuck on my eating Chinese food. "You won't be seventeen years old forever. You keep eating like that, you'll end up with high blood pressure. It runs in our family."

I turned to Dad. "Did you hear anything about a

giant bird sighting from last night?"

"Nothing on TV or the newspaper," he replied. He piled a stack of french toast on a serving plate and brought it over before sitting down with us. "You think it was one of those giant vultures?"

"That's what Brandon thought," I said. "Shannon swore that it wasn't a bird."

Dad asked, "What did she think it was?"

Mom had finally zeroed-in on our conversation, and she stared at me, waiting for my answer. I took a deep breath, not sure how to word my response correctly and not sound like I was insane.

"She said it looked like a man."

"A man?" Mom put her tablet down. "With wings? Like an angel?"

I knew right away that I had made a terrible mistake. "Not like an angel. Or maybe, yes. I don't know. I saw wings for sure. It was dark, but Shannon can see from really far away, and she said that she noticed the creature had feet and hands."

"Maybe it's time for Shannon to get her eyes checked." Mom looked unconvinced and a little concerned about my mental health. "It was probably just a big hawk."

Dad slid a plate in my direction. "Your mother's right. Hawks can get pretty big. Vultures too."

There was no way to explain everything I had experienced. Seeing the flying creature was just part of it. The entire night was so messed up. Otherworldly. I couldn't get my parents to understand how all four of us had also felt a sense of dread and panic. How we felt like we had been sent to another dimension for just those fifteen minutes. Mom and Dad would probably just say that I was brainwashing myself with all the science fiction I read and watched.

"If it was a bird, it was the biggest bird in the world," I said before stabbing two slices of french toast with my fork. "I was just curious if other people had reported it, that's all."

Mom pointed to the folded newspaper on the table. "Nothing here at all about a giant bird sighting."

I was getting nowhere, so I changed the subject. "I think I will need another pair of jeans, Mom."

"I've got a coupon for Kochel's," Mom said before taking a swig of her coffee. "We can go after we're done eating. I might have to show a house later this afternoon."

I ignored the uneasy feeling settling in the pit of my stomach, hoping a home-cooked breakfast would ease it. But even after I had finished my plate, I still felt bothered. I left the table and washed my plate and fork.

"Go get dressed, alright?" Mom called out after I had left the kitchen.

I turned to give her a quick "okay" before heading back to my bedroom. I decided to glance at some of the online message boards and the UFO Network website before leaving. Somebody else had to have seen the flying creature last night.

After going to various conspiracy and UFO websites, I had come up empty-handed. I texted the others to give them a quick update before getting dressed and heading out the door to go back-to-school shopping with Mom.

"Senior year." Mom veered the family SUV into Kochel's parking lot. "It's an important time."

I shrugged. "Yeah."

Mom was gearing up for yet one of our mother-son talks. They consisted mostly of her talking and me not saying a word. She had grown up poor, so I understood why she was so concerned with my future. I had a lot of decisions to make this year, and I dreaded having to make them.

"Have you been giving thought as to which school is your top choice?" she asked me.

She never had gone on to college, which made her push me to be studious. I was fortunate that school work was never difficult for me. In fact, I hadn't given much effort to get a 3.8 GPA and a 34 on my ACT. I was sure to snag a few big scholarships to schools in Missouri and Illinois, and Dad had gone to Mizzou. It was about two hours away, which was about as far as Mom wanted me to be.

"Yeah. A lot." I sighed, preparing for her lecture.

Mom found a parking spot far away from the doors. She liked to walk. "We can schedule another visit to Mizzou this fall. It would be a great time to see the campus with all the kids coming back to school."

Maybe it was because I didn't want to make the wrong decision. Or perhaps it was the thought that Elijah would be having to figure out which college to attend if he was alive today. Either way, I was sure that our impending birthday was what put me in my annual funk.

"Sounds good, Mom."

"I know this is a tough time." Mom killed the engine. "It's always difficult for all of us."

I wanted to open the door and go shopping for new jeans. I wasn't in the mood to talk about anything related to my dead brother.

"I think you should see Ms. Kim again," she continued. "You always needed a little extra help this time of year. You've got a lot on your plate. Last year of high school. College decisions. Your birthday."

Mom meant well, and nothing I could have said would stop her worrying. "I'll be fine. If I feel like I'm losing it, you'll be the first to know."

Mom was never one to let things go. She was the queen of beating a dead horse. "There is nothing wrong with having to take the right medications to keep from getting too depressed. You understand?"

"Yeah." I turned to give her my very best reassuring look. "I understand."

She looked unconvinced, but she pulled the keys from the ignition and opened her door. "Good. Let's get you some new jeans. Maybe a jacket."

It had always been impossible to sleep the night before the first day of school. A big part of it was the fact that my body wasn't used to sleeping before ten o'clock after having stayed up late all summer. Anxiety and nervousness always went along with starting a new school year. But I was a senior this year, and I had some blow-off classes on my schedule, finally. Other than AP calculus and physics, I was taking a bunch of fun electives.

I eventually started to drift. I had never been a big dreamer. Even though we all dreamed, I was one of those who never remembered them. If I hadn't understood some of the science of sleep, I would have thought that I never dreamed at all.

But that night, I had my first true nightmare.

The first of many to come.

The sky was blood-red, and the moon looked as big and bright as the sun. I was in my car driving home when a deafening bang on the roof of my Camry scared the hell out of me. For sure, something had fallen and dented my car.

My initial thought was that Dad was going to kill me. He had dropped full coverage on my car and went with liability. Any damage to it wouldn't be covered.

I pulled over, and my heart slammed against my ribs. When I got out, I found two massive dents on the roof but no evidence of what had actually hit my car. I looked up, wondering if someone had dropped something from the overpass. Nothing.

With the help of the bright moonlight, I inspected the dents and noticed that they looked like claw prints. They reminded me of Bigfoot footprints, and they were embedded perfectly in the metal of my car's roof.

The sound of swooshing overhead made me duck, and I hurried back inside my car in case the sky was falling. I locked the door and tried to start my car, but it wouldn't turn. I was sure that my heart was going to explode inside my chest.

It was as if the moon had been unplugged, and everything grew dark. The red sky continued to swirl, but the darkness swallowed everything up. It was so black, I couldn't see the road anymore. I pressed my face up against the side window, and it looked like a tornado was about to descend right on top of me. I gripped my steering wheel, waiting for the storm to suck me up. Instead, two red spherical eyes stared back at me through my car's windshield.

It made no sense, but I knew they were eyes. They glowed like fire. When my vision adjusted to the darkness, I was able to make out the creature's silhouette, especially its wings. Soon, I discerned its somewhat humanoid form.

But none of that mattered. I couldn't stop looking into its red eyes. They never blinked or wavered but kept me under the weight of their stare. At that moment, I felt a million different emotions at once. Despair, fear, and grief.

I jolted myself awake.

My body was covered in sweat, and I used my thin sheets as a towel. Part of me was still stuck in the world of nightmares. It took all of my strength to yank myself back into reality. I made a mental note of the creature's appearance from my nightmare. My conscious side fully woke up, acknowledging that the previous night's sighting of the giant bird creature was the source of my nightmare. But the strangest image from my dream had nothing to do with the monster.

Just before I had forced myself to wake up, I saw Elijah's nine-year-old face. The foggy image appeared and disappeared in a flash. At first, I thought I was looking into a mirror, but I could feel that it was my brother looking right at me. His mouth had been open, as if he wanted to say something to me, but I had ripped myself out of sleep before he could say it.

I got up from bed and pulled my ceiling fan's chain until it was on full-blast. There was no getting any sleep after having such a scary and strange nightmare. I lay mostly awake, drifting off many times until the sun finally came up.

CHAPTER 3

Despite not getting any sleep, the first day of school went without any issues. Luckily, Shannon and I had the same lunch period, although Brandon and Dylan ate later. We didn't talk about the giant bird-man when we sat at our regular table, next to the large cafeteria windows. Instead, we caught up on all the everyday fun gossip. With this being our senior year, we were nostalgic about our favorite and least favorite teachers.

That night at dinner, things continued to go normally. Mom asked if I was still going to be president of the school's Science Fiction Club, and I told her that, of course, I intended to run it again. She disapproved, as she thought it wasn't scholarly enough. Dad had to remind her that I had already received scholarship offers from four different schools, so there was no need for me to pad my resume with extracurricular stuff.

The second day of school, however, was far from normal.

Human relations class was filled with all seniors. Mrs. Massey was our teacher, and she could have had her own talk show. The woman had such an amazing personality, which held our attention. Sure, this was going to be an easy class that we all signed up for to help pass the time away during our last year in high school, but she vowed to teach us some real-life stuff that we needed before we embarked out into the real world.

She talked about our first unit, which dealt with different personality types. Mrs. Massey discussed how many of us were already dealing with all kinds of personality types at our part-time jobs. Learning how to handle all of these temperaments would help us be successful.

I had been doodling all hour, half-paying attention to Mrs. Massey's lesson, when I started day dreaming. At first, a low murmuring vibrated in my right ear. It sounded like someone was whispering gibberish. I turned in that direction to confirm that no one had snuck up from behind me to freak me out. The faint mumbling grew in volume until I swore someone had to be playing a cruel joke on me.

For my first two years of high school, I had been

bullied a lot. I was scrawny and probably looked pretty weak to all the tough guys at school. On top of that, I was a big sci-fi geek. An outcast. They picked on me almost every day, short of actually beating me up. Freshman year, they stuck me in a locker and sprayed hairspray into the slits to make me gag. Sophomore year in gym, they yanked down my shorts every chance they got.

Junior year was when I was elected president of the Science Fiction Club, and I think that's when I started to become confident and comfortable in my own skin. I wasn't as small either, but I felt like I could handle myself if those idiots tried anything. It was a big turning point for me, and sure enough, the bullying stopped.

Who would try to pull a fast one on me now? I was surrounded by a bunch of girls. There were only four other guys in the class, and they weren't the kind to pull pranks like this. I couldn't understand what the voice was saying, but I thought it sounded like a male voice. It might have even said my name.

Just before I passed out, my vision became filled with static. It was as if I had gone blind. All I saw was white, black, and gray lines dancing in my field of vision. And in the middle of all that static, the image of a flying monster took shape slowly, like a fog transforming into something solid.

It looked exactly like the winged creature in my

nightmare two nights ago. It got bigger and bigger until its red eyes dominated my vision. It unleashed a screeching sound, which replaced the faint murmuring in my right ear. The high-pitched wailing grew until I couldn't stand it anymore. My head started to spin, and then everything went blank.

A hot, searing sensation on my left arm brought me to consciousness. When I opened my eyes, I found myself hovering in the air, or so I thought at first. I lay on a gurney, surrounded by a bunch of familiar faces and two strange ones.

"You okay Jonah?" one of the strangers asked me.

It was a guy with stale breath. I wanted to ask him if he wanted a Tic Tac, but I remembered that I didn't have any with me.

"Yeah." It took some effort to turn my stiff neck to see Mrs. Massey coming up to me.

"We called your parents," she said to me. "They will meet you at the hospital."

"Hospital?" I shook myself fully awake. The paramedics had started an IV, and they were wheeling me out into the hallway. "I'm fine. I don't need to go to the hospital."

The other students had congregated on the far side of the room and stared at me with concerned eyes. Mrs.

Massey took my hand and gave it a good squeeze. "They're going to take you to St. Paul just to make sure. Your parents will already be there by the time you arrive. Always better to be safe than sorry."

It was no use protesting. I had passed out in the middle of class, so they probably wanted to make sure I wasn't on drugs or suddenly had epilepsy. No way was I going to tell them I had hallucinated about a flying monster and its banshee-like screaming that knocked me out. They'd lock me up in a padded room for sure.

"I'll have someone take your backpack down to the office," Mrs. Massey continued as she followed me out into the hall. "You can pick it up when you come back to school."

I tried my best to return her smile. "Thanks."

Saying Mom wasn't very good at dealing with any kind of emergency was an understatement. She was already hitting me with all kinds of questions when they rolled my gurney into the ER. Dad, on the other hand, was his normal, calm self.

"The doctor will have to examine him first, ma'am," the paramedic with the stink breath said to her. "But he will be just fine."

"What's wrong with him?" Mom asked him.

The pair of EMTs glanced at each other before the lady replied, "He might be a little dehydrated. But they'll have to run some tests to find out exactly what happened."

Mom started to interrogate me, but Dad got between us. We waited in silence in the hallway for what felt like hours. When we finally got to a room, the nurse took my blood pressure, which was probably sky high, and checked my other vitals before leaving.

"I give you a full water bottle every day before school, and you never drink it," Mom said through tight lips. "See what can happen when you don't drink enough water?"

Dad shook his head. "The paramedics don't know for sure if Jonah's dehydrated. It was just a guess."

The same nurse returned and asked my parents a ton of health questions, which seemed to amp up Mom even more. I could almost hear the paranoia-filled thoughts swirling in her brain. Epilepsy? Heart condition? Brain tumor? A million ailments could take away the only son she had left, and there was no talking sense to her. Mom had lost one child already, and the thought of losing me was why she was always so overprotective.

"Dr. Chen will be in to see him," the nurse said to Mom and Dad. "It will be just a minute."

She gave me a reassuring smile before exiting the room.

Dad came over to my bed and leaned in. "Is there anything you need to tell us? Anything at all?"

"I'm not doing drugs, Dad," I replied.

He threw his hands up. "I wasn't implying you were. We know you've got a lot on your mind. We just want to make sure you're not feeling overwhelmed."

If Mom wasn't in the room, I might have said something about what happened to me before I blacked out. Maybe talking about having visions of a winged creature screaming wasn't such a good idea since I was in a hospital. St. Paul did have a psych ward. I'd end up in there for sure.

"I am overwhelmed," I said truthfully. "But I don't think I'm stressed out enough to make me pass out like that in the middle of class."

"Dehydration is very dangerous," Mom said as she wagged her pointy finger at me. "People underestimate how important drinking water is."

I closed my eyes and let my head sink into the pillows. "I know, Mom."

After running a bunch of tests that required me to give up what felt like half of my blood supply, I was allowed to go home. Everything checked out just fine. I had no heart arrhythmias, and my glucose levels and blood pressure were normal. Dr. Chen said I was probably just dehydrated and stressed out.

We got home just before eleven, and Mom said I didn't have to go to school the next day if I didn't feel like it. Her show of mercy surprised me, and I decided right there and then I was going to stay home. I promised to drink water throughout the day and to try to get as much rest as I could.

Without having to ask, I was sure Mom and Dad were going to set up an appointment for me to see Ms. Kim. It wasn't that I felt the counselor was horrible. In fact, I found Ms. Kim's sessions helpful, but I didn't like all the introspection involved. Everything revolved around the loss of Elijah, it seemed. I was already very aware of it, so going in to talk to the counselor just to rehash old news felt like a waste of my time.

Mom and Dad went straight for their bedroom, but I lingered in the kitchen. I sat at the table, trying to recall everything that had happened before I had blacked out. The images came back with such clarity, I thought I might faint again.

The winged creature's red, glowing eyes haunted me the most. It made no sense, though. What Shannon had seen had wings, feet, and hands, but she made no mention of it having red eyes. My imagination was playing crazy tricks on me. I didn't want to admit it, but maybe I did need some serious psychiatric help.

Dad was always the first up and out the door. He didn't have a long commute at all, as the company he worked at was only a couple miles away. Regardless, he was one of the top dogs there, so he felt obligated to get to work early.

I came down to grab a water bottle to show Mom I was making sure to stay hydrated. Sure enough, just as I had finished filling it up, she walked into the kitchen with a scowl on her face.

"Are you sure you're okay here at home?" she asked me.

"I'm just going to take it easy, just like I promised last night," I replied. "Drink lots of water. Watch *The Price is Right* and maybe a few trashy talk shows."

Mom gathered some of her paperwork and placed it inside her leather briefcase. "I will come back with some lunch. You have anything in particular in mind?"

"Maybe just some Bread Cafe." I guzzled some water to put her mind at ease. "You know what I like."

She walked over to me and touched my face. Mom was never one to show much affection, although she did have her moments. "If you need anything, just call me."

"I will."

Mom grabbed her car keys from the small table

near the laundry room and went through the garage to her SUV.

I hurried back to my room when it dawned on me that my friends were probably worried about me. My jeans lay crumpled on the floor, and I reached into the right pocket to retrieve my phone.

Sure enough, I had dozens of text messages from the gang, mostly from Shannon.

I rushed a single text to Brandon, Dylan, and Shannon to let them know I was alright. My battery was about to give out, so I sent the message and plugged the phone back into the cord next to my computer. I thought about doing a more thorough sweep online to see if anyone had reported seeing the giant flying bird, but I decided against it.

After finishing off what was left of my water bottle, I strolled through the kitchen into the living room. I plopped myself down on the couch and turned on the television. The morning news shows were still on, and there was nothing much on TV yet. I let the droning of the news anchors become a backdrop, and I let my mind and body relax. Maybe it was because I still had some sleeping to catch up on. Or the soft fluffy couch was just too comfortable. But without effort, I dozed off.

The crimson sky swirled above me, like molten lava bubbling and getting ready to pour down onto the earth. Directly in front of me was a familiar playground. It looked exactly like the one at Corazon Park not too far from our house. I had avoided the park since Elijah's death, but now here I was, standing directly in front of where he had died over eight years ago.

I looked at the palms of my hands. My stubby fingers wiggled. These were the hands of a nine-year-old. My conscious mind told me I was dreaming once again, but I let the dream play itself out.

It was pointless to even try, but I looked for Elijah. On the day he died, Mom had dressed us up in matching outfits: blue Nike t-shirts with gray sweatpants. Hundreds of kids swarmed around the playground, so I scanned the area, looking for a kid wearing the identical clothes I had on. At the height of my frustration, all the other children magically vanished.

I loved to hide inside the tunnel slide, so that was the first placed I sought. I climbed up the metal stairs and stuck my head into the tubular opening, but Elijah wasn't in there. That was a stupid thing to do, since I knew he had gone into the woods with the stranger. I was about to slide down the tall pole and run to the restroom where Mom had gone, but the sound of flapping wings overhead made me stop.

At first, I thought the creature looked just like a pterodactyl. One of the first books I had ever purchased at a book fair was a huge book of dinosaurs. The pictures looked so real, and I made Dad teach me how to pronounce every single creature. When the monster high above me plunged towards the ground, I knew it wasn't one of those prehistoric beasts.

Its red eyes grew brighter and zeroed in on me. I felt as if it could somehow read my thoughts. Once again, my conscious mind intervened for just a second to remind me this was only a dream. Panic rose up from my throat, and I slid down the pole to take cover.

I scurried underneath the giant playground structure and covered my head. After waiting several moments, I peeked to see if the creature had left. Any moment now, Mom would be coming out of the restroom about fifty yards away to find Elijah gone.

I wanted to sprint towards the restroom and tell her what had happened to my brother, but I was too scared to leave the safety of my hiding place. I craned my neck to see if the monster was still flying up in the red sky, but I couldn't find any trace of it. I willed my body to go, and I broke into a mad dash towards the small brick building where Mom had gone into just a few minutes ago.

Without having to look, I knew the winged creature was following me. I could hear its massive wings flapping. Its ear-splitting scream pierced my eardrums. I didn't want to look into its red eyes again, so I just kept running. I commanded my little nine-year-old legs to take me to the restroom building as fast as they could.

Something struck the back of my head and I went down. It felt as if a bowling ball had been hurled at me, and my entire body ached. Was my neck broken? Had the creature struck me with one of its talons?

With my eyes closed, I felt the world spinning all around me. I tried to move, but I was paralyzed. Maybe my spine had been snapped, and I was crippled for life. My conscious mind broke through yet again to tell me not to panic and I was not crippled in real life. It was no good. I started to cry, hoping Mom could hear me.

I forced my eyes to open and hovering directly above me was the creature. My vision was blurry, as if I had been hit so hard in the head my sight had been affected. I tried rubbing my eyes, but my hands and arms still wouldn't budge.

The last thing I saw was the monster's red eyes. Unblinking. Penetrating. I woke up, but I was still paralyzed. My mouth wouldn't even open to let out a scream. The living room ceiling fan was on full blast, and I watched the blades go round and round. I was fully awake. So why couldn't I move?

My chest heaved. Beads of sweat slid down my face from my forehead. I was having a panic attack. With all the power I had, I forced myself to take deep breaths. It felt like hours until I was able to control my breathing. Eventually, the sensation in my feet and my hands returned.

I let the wind from the ceiling fan caress my sweat-soaked body. I tried to make myself fully aware of the living room as best I could. The TV was on, and it sounded like a newscast was still playing. Sunlight entered the large sliding glass windows that led to the backyard. Someone was mowing their lawn far away. Yes, I was in the real world again.

When I raised my arm, I was relieved to see my hand had returned to normal. My long, bony fingers did a quick dance, and soon I was able to sit up. I wiped the film of perspiration on my forehead with the back of my hand.

My legs slid off the couch. I sat with my head in my hands for a long time before I stood up. The panic attack passed, and I relished the calm that eventually replaced the fear.

I went towards the kitchen to satisfy my thirst. My tongue felt dry and swollen. I had every intention of drinking three gallons of water and then watching *The Price is Right* to further solidify my existence in the real and mundane world.

CHAPTER 4

"**Y**OU WANT US to go to Corazon Park?" Shannon asked before taking a bite from her sandwich. "I don't get it."

The scent of pizza and janitorial disinfectant was enough to make a normal person sick, but the entire student body had become immune to the offending stench. The tub of french fries in front of me actually looked appealing, but it was probably only because I was starving.

No one around us in the cafeteria was eavesdropping, but I looked around just to make sure. "Yesterday at home, I had a weird dream about the playground."

Shannon let out a sarcastic chuckle. "I dream about Captain America, and you don't see me wanting to join the army to get close to him. So what?"

"I can't explain." I grabbed three french fries and

stuffed them in my mouth before continuing. "It wasn't just a dream. For some reason, I just feel like I'm supposed to go back there. Maybe it's part of my…healing after all these years."

"You've stayed away from there for a good reason," Shannon said. "Are you sure you want to go back?"

I was going to tell her about the flying creature in my dream and the nightmare about the monster flying over my car, but I decided not to. Just wanting to go to Corazon Park was enough for her.

"I'm sure."

"Alright. I'm in." Shannon put her hand on my shoulder. "If it will help you get better, then I'm all for it. I'll text Brandon and Dylan to meet us at your car after sixth period. You really had us freaked when we heard about you passing out in class."

I shrugged. "It's no big deal. It wasn't a seizure or anything serious like that. Just stress and dehydration."

Shannon slid her unopened bottle of water my way. "Here. Just in case."

"You sound like my mother," I said as I took the water.

"Just without the accent," she quipped.

Brandon tapped the back of my headrest. "What you're

saying is that this is literally therapeutic."

I turned onto the street that led directly to the park. "Yes...I think. Or maybe it'll make me want to hang myself."

Shannon elbowed me. "Don't joke about that."

"I think it's a good thing," Dylan said from the back seat. He tapped his knobby knees with both hands. "Maybe it's a sign you're ready to completely move on. You know, get past Elijah's death."

"That's right, Dr. Phil," Brandon said. "My uncle has PTSD from the Gulf War. I don't think taking a trip back to Afghanistan is going to do him any good." He leaned back in his seat. "I hope you know what you're doing."

The four of us sat in silence as I steered the car along the winding road. Ancient trees created a dark canopy, and it felt like nighttime all of a sudden. The narrow road went into a steep decline. I rode my brakes all the way down until I made a sharp turn into one of the park's entrances.

This part of Corazon had a couple tennis courts, a giant metal pavilion that was often rented out for parties, a small brick building with restrooms, and an elaborate playground.

At night, couples would come up here and make out in front of the amazing view of the lake. Today, only a couple of families were at the playground. Many people didn't come to this part of the park since it was easy to drive right past the hidden entrance. Almost everyone else was down by the lake.

I parked near the restrooms and turned off the engine. My pulse started to race, and I knew I would have to get a grip if I was to avoid having a panic attack. Shannon took my hand and gave me a reassuring look, which helped. When the worst of it passed, I opened my car door. The others followed.

"I think I've only been up to this part of the park once in the last nine years," Brandon said as he stepped onto the pavement. "Company picnic. I think the big pavilion down by the lake was already reserved, so they stuck us up here."

Shannon meandered towards the playground, leading the way. "Nothing's changed."

Dylan went to the tube slide and knocked on the hard metal. "How the heck did we fit inside this thing?"

"You never fit," I said. My feet sank into the brown pebbles covering the ground. "Yeah, this is pretty weird."

Brandon crept over and studied my face. "You don't look like you're on the verge of a nervous breakdown. Yet."

The palms of my hands became damp, and I made myself take deep breaths to keep myself together. I took uneasy steps towards the playground until I came to the pair of swings. A little girl pumped her legs until she got enough momentum to easily go as high as my head. Her father watched from the park bench on the edge of the playground.

"You okay?" Shannon whispered.

I imagined Elijah in the swing, giggling and laughing so hard, his face turned red. He would swing as high as he could and then jump off while yelling "Superman!" I gave Shannon a quick nod before going to an empty bench to sit down.

Dylan and Brandon continued walking past the playground and went to the pavilion. Its giant roof reminded me of a flying saucer, and the pair stared out at the fantastic view of the entire manmade lake.

Shannon sat next to me. "It's not so bad, is it?"

I was about to tell her "no" when a shadow flew above us. We both held our breaths and jerked our faces upwards, only to see a large hawk gliding over the trees. Both of us expelled a deep sigh of relief before laughing at each other.

"Have you told anyone?" I asked her. "About what we saw the other night?"

She shook her head. "I don't tell my mom a whole lot in the first place. You?"

"I sort of did," I replied. "But my parents blew me off. I didn't get a good chance to really check online much. Just here and there, but I've come up with nothing. No one's reported seeing a giant flying bird-man-thing."

"I know you guys think I was just seeing things," Shannon said. "But I am one hundred percent sure I saw its hands and feet. Arms and legs. Reminded me of Hawk Man. Just without the big-ass mace."

I turned up to the perfect blue sky again. A majestic hawk circled above the trees before flying away. "Did you see its face? Maybe its eyes?"

"Nope." Shannon bent down, picked up a rock, and threw it into the grass. "It was too far away, even for my eagle eyes. I don't even want to think about what its face might look like. I imagine it has a long beak and razor-sharp teeth. Yellow eyes."

The creature had red eyes, but I wasn't about to explain to Shannon how I had been having messed up dreams about it. Coming back to the park was enough.

"You holding up okay?" Shannon asked.

"This wasn't as tough as I thought it was going to be," I replied. "Maybe enough time has passed, and I don't have to keep acting crazy around this time of year."

Shannon understood. "Oh. Your birthday."

"It's weird. Elijah's been gone now just as long as he was alive. I often try to imagine what he'd look like today."

"Look in the mirror," Shannon said.

I allowed myself to laugh. "Just with darker eyes."

Shannon scrunched up her nose. "Hard to imagine eyes darker than yours. I've seen all your old family photos up at your house, but I always get you two mixed up in pictures."

"Yeah, Elijah had darker brown eyes," I said. "It's pretty subtle, and you really can't see it in pictures."

"Gotcha." Shannon smiled. "Scientists say identical twins are clones. So, with you and Elijah, a part of him is always going to be with you, right?"

I nodded. Shannon always had a way of putting things in perspective. "I can't help but wonder what Elijah would be like today. Dad said we had such different personalities. I was shy, but Elijah was the loud one."

"Do you feel guilty?" Shannon looked like she regretted her question the moment it left her lips. She pushed a stray strand of her brown hair away from her face, which meant she was nervous.

"Yeah," I replied. "I know Mom does. That's probably why she's such a worrier. Part of it is her personality, but she feels guilty. She went to the restroom for just a minute. The man took Elijah into the woods through the trail. I went to go tell her, and when I went back to the playground..."

Shannon stared at the little girl on the swing. "It's not your or your mom's fault."

I stood up and stretched. "I know. My logical side understands it all, but I can't help how I feel. I think there's always going to be guilt there."

"So now what?" Shannon left the bench and

stepped towards my car. "You ready to get out of here?"

Brandon and Dylan were still sitting at one of the picnic tables underneath the flying saucer pavilion. Brandon had his phone out, as usual, but Dylan stared at the lake below.

"I think I want to go down there," I said.

Shannon's brown eyes widened, a sharp crease forming between her thin brows. "The lake? Are you sure? Coming here was already a huge step forward. Maybe going down to the lake is too much for you."

After graduating, I was going to be leaving town for college. I wanted to leave all my trauma and fear behind. I would leave St. Louis a better person, ready to move forward in my life. The playground was a monumental achievement, but going to the lake would be the ultimate test.

Standing near the place where Elijah's body had been found might have pushed me over the edge, but I had to take that chance. I had to regain my sanity.

I pulled into a busy parking lot, and we found ourselves surrounded by joggers, bicyclists, and skaters making their way around the brilliant lake. Dylan and Brandon got out first, but they waited for me at the front of my car. Shannon looked as traumatized as I felt. She opened her door and sat there for a long time before getting out.

My hands tightened around the steering wheel, and it took all my energy to finally let go. Once I pushed my door open and stepped out, I was greeted by a cool wind whipping off the surface of the lake.

It was an absolute gorgeous day. Kids ran around with their parents, dogs happily jogged with their owners, and someone's stereo was blasting out some crazy heavy metal music.

When I gazed onto the glittering surface of the water, panic seized me. My lungs failed to expand, and my breath got caught in my throat. Shannon seemed to sense this, and she reached out to give me a comforting pat on my back.

"We can go now," Shannon whispered.

My head nodded slightly, but I told her, "No. I need to do this."

Dylan and Brandon walked from the parking lot over to a picnic table just on the edge of the sand that surrounded the lake. I took several steps towards them but stopped when a skater zoomed by. Shannon took my arm and led me over the blacktop path onto the sandy area.

"You alright, man?" Dylan asked as he ran his hand through his spiky, blond hair. "Maybe this wasn't such a good idea."

I felt my knees tremble, and I hurried to take a seat

across from Brandon. "I'm good. Just need to catch my breath."

Brandon stared out into the water. He had known me and Elijah since kindergarten, so this had to have been tough for him too. He let out a long, deep sigh. "I've been here at least a dozen times since Elijah died, and it still messes with me."

Dylan and Shannon hadn't known Elijah in grade school, but they remained silent as if they were keeping a silent vigil for my lost brother. Even though they didn't know him, it meant a lot to me that they were there. My hands kept shaking, so I folded them together in an effort to calm down.

"I never really asked you this before," Brandon said as he leaned towards me. "Sometimes, I get confused when I think about us being kids. It was Elijah who was a class clown, right? He got in trouble all the time for talking."

"That's right," I said.

Brandon's already serious face turned even more grim. "Ok, so after Elijah passed, you became more talkative. When you were little, you barely spoke. In fact, we used to say Elijah was the only one you talked to. You know how they say twins create their own languages and can even feel each other's pain and stuff, even when they're thousands of miles apart? With you two being so close, did you experience that kind of stuff?"

I thought about Brandon's question for a long time before replying. "Shannon and I were kind of talking about that a few minutes ago. Yeah, I think so. For a long time, I couldn't sleep or eat, since Elijah was always at my side for everything. Mom said we were like yin and yang, complete opposites as individuals, and together, we made a whole person. After Elijah died, I assumed some of his personality traits to keep a part of him alive in a way."

The day after Elijah's disappearance, the police came to our house to tell us they had found his body. The look on the first officer told me all I needed to hear. At first, Mom and Dad looked confused. I kept my distance, staying at the threshold between the kitchen and the living room, and they kept blankly staring at the cop as if they couldn't comprehend what he was telling them.

The way Mom cried out shocked me. She was a tough woman, and I had never seen her cry before. She had collapsed and started wailing on the floor. Dad had to pick her up and drag her over to the couch. I ran upstairs and planted my wet face into Elijah's bed and stayed there for a long time.

Losing Elijah was like losing half of my identity. I had wondered if my own heart would suddenly stop beating. Could I exist in this world without my twin brother? He was like my other half, and without him, I would never be whole again. That would explain why

I had become outgoing like Elijah. It was my way of connecting with him.

"Mom liked to buy us identical clothing, just to confuse the hell out of people," I said. When I chuckled, the others smiled along with me. "I remember going into Elijah's closet and wearing his favorite outfits. Made no sense, since I had the exact same clothes in my closet."

Dylan knocked on the picnic table nervously. "Is this helping you?" he asked me.

"It's not easy, but this is good," I finally said.

Shannon said, "Whenever you're ready, we can go."

I looked her in the eyes, then turned to the others. "I'm ready."

We grabbed a quick dinner consisting of cheeseburgers and fries before I dropped the others off, one by one. Shannon lived closest to me, so she was last. Hardly anyone had spoken while we ate, and during the car ride back, we all were lost in our thoughts. When I pulled up to Shannon's small ranch house, she flashed me a smile before getting out.

I didn't feel like going home yet. I texted Mom to tell her I was at Shannon's house and I'd be back either just before or right after dark. Of course, she wanted to know if I was feeling OK, and I told her I had been drinking lots of water all day.

Not sure of where to go, I drove in circles for a few minutes before deciding to drive to Elijah's and my favorite place, the old toy store. It was a good fifteen minutes away, and I had to contend with the late rush hour traffic. Even from afar, I could tell it was no longer open.

When did the toy store close? I could have sworn it was bustling with shoppers just last Christmas season, but I had lost track of time. It looked like the store had shuttered years ago. The building was under construction as if a new store would be opening in its place.

I parked in the empty lot and sat there, reliving the day Elijah had been taken from us. For at least an hour, I felt like I was nine years old again. The fear and anger felt just as fresh as it did back then. A hot tear escaped my left eye when the memory of Mom's screaming filled my head. Hyperthymesia had its drawbacks.

My thoughts turned to Mom and Dad. Naturally, their focus had been on me and my well-being after Elijah's death. We might as well have been Siamese twins, always together. Dad said I had trouble sleeping for at least six months. I never really stopped to think about what they had gone through. It must have been horrible losing a child.

I wondered if they relived it every day like I did.

The sun sank below the horizon. It was time to leave to avoid Mom worrying more than she already did. I started the engine and left the abandoned toy store. It had been a place of great memories, and now, it was just an abandoned, old shell. What about the store's employees? What were they doing now? I hope they had found a job, a better one, after the toy store closed. How difficult had it been for them to move on with their lives?

I shook my head of such stupid thoughts. I turned on the radio to try to jolt my brain back into the real world. Streetlights flickered on, and I turned on my headlights.

With only a few more blocks to drive until I reached home, I sat at a stop sign just inside my subdivision. At first, I thought maybe I was on the verge of another panic attack. My forehead got really cold, and sweat formed in my armpits and on my lower back. The need to get out of the car was so compelling, I pulled over and killed the engine.

I stepped out of my car and hurried to the sidewalk, trying to get a grip. The houses to my right were all dark, and to my left was the common ground area. A small playground was going to be built there, but the subdivision association never got around to it. It made no sense to put one up, since there were hardly any little kids around anymore.

My head began to throb, and I thought maybe I

should have listened to Mom and actually drank tons of water. I didn't hear a voice in my head or anything, but I needed to look up. So, I did.

And that's when the flying creature streamed across the sky, high above the trees.

CHAPTER 5

IT FELT LIKE I watched the flying monster glide over the subdivision for a good five minutes, but it was probably over in seconds. I thought about texting a message to the others, but there wasn't enough time. The creature soared higher up, and I noted it was heading towards the industrial complex where Dad worked.

I jumped in my car and tried my best not to speed as I drove towards Dad's work. Maybe a few employees lingered at the office after hours, but it was unlikely. Traffic was starting to lighten up, and I turned onto the side road toward the part of town known as Commerce City. There had to be a hundred businesses in this entire section, if not more. In fact, it had its very own zip code.

Dad was the chief financial officer for a company that distributed some kind of plastic wrap used to secure shipments on pallets. They were a small operation, fewer than fifty employees, but their building was gigantic since it stored so many huge rolls of plastic inside.

I kept trying to glance upwards, but it was impossible to search for the monster without wrecking the car. The road narrowed and curved widely with small and large commercial buildings on either side me. Dad's building was at the very end of the main strip, and with no other cars on the road, I gunned the engine.

The car nearly took to the air when I hit the bump of pavement at the entrance to the empty parking lot. The yellow lights lit the area, and it looked deserted all around me. Out of habit, I parked the car neatly inside the lines and jumped out.

Darkness dominated the sky, and at the very edge of the western horizon, the faintest orange glow of sunlight remained. The landfill was directly across the street from Dad's building, and the putrid stench made me gag. It had been nasty all summer, but it was a million times worse at this close range. The real fear was the radioactive garbage underground and how it could give people rare brain tumors and cancers. Mom always brought up how they should move the company far away from the landfill. She was right.

The sharp odor alone was enough for me to shut the landfill down and get it cleaned up. I didn't understand how Dad could stand it. There was talk last year of the company's owner and president actually moving their operations elsewhere, but nothing ever came of it, much to Mom's frustration.

My eyes watered, and I had to swallow to keep my burger and fries down. After my eyesight adjusted to the night, I thought I was seeing things. The creature's wings were much larger than I remembered, and I could make out what looked like legs. It circled directly over the landfill, like a buzzard waiting for its prey to die before picking the flesh from the bones.

Time stood still, and I watched the creature for a long time. Once in a while, I'd look around to see if anyone else was seeing this. I got out my phone, but I knew taking video wouldn't work. It was way too dark.

It seemed to lose altitude, but I couldn't get a good look at its head. Did it have red eyes? Was it drawn to the stink of the landfill? It swooped in low and disappeared behind a mountain of covered waste.

I waited for a good ten minutes for the creature to take to the skies again. My mind replayed what I had just seen, and I slapped my own face just to make sure I wasn't dreaming. I was about to get back in the car and get home before Mom called the police to search for her missing son, when a heavy dread overcame me.

Panic attack? No. This was exactly how I felt that night we first saw the winged monster. Apparently, all four of us had the same uneasy sensation just before we saw the flying beast. Why did this thing make our "Spidey Sense" tingle like this?

I opened the door to my car, but I suddenly couldn't move. It was as if someone had hit me with an ice ray gun. I knew a full-blown panic attack was on its way. I was able to close my eyes, and I did my best to control my breathing. My paralysis wouldn't allow me to turn around and look, but I knew someone was behind me.

In all my life, I had never prayed so hard for a cop to accost me. I didn't hear footsteps or anything, but I could feel his presence. I wanted to call out to whoever was coming towards me, but my mouth wouldn't move. I opened my eyes and was about to ask him if he had also seen the giant birdman flying around the landfill, when my body broke its frozen curse, and I whirled around to face him.

A pair of eyes as red as the sun hovered just a few feet in front of me.

The last time I had wet my pants, Mom said I was five years old at the mall and she wasn't able to get me to the restroom in time. The instant I realized the winged creature stood next to my car, I nearly lost all control of my bodily functions. If I had peed my pants, I wouldn't have known it anyway, as I had no sensation in my legs.

My whole body became numb again.

Its eyes were too bright for me to look directly at them, but I tried to make out the rest of it. The thing easily stood seven or eight feet tall. It was a true monster. It had two arms, but I couldn't perceive its hands in the dark. I imagined it had Wolverine-like steel claws. My gaze fell downwards, and sure enough, it had legs.

Shannon's eagle eyes had never failed her, and I felt stupid for even doubting what she'd seen.

I wanted to see the beast's face, but I knew the hot glow of its eyes would burn my retinas. The sound of dry leaves rustling surrounded me. Had the sound come from its wings? My brain did its best to try to make sense of what was happening. But my instincts told me I was in the presence of something not of this world.

I had seen enough alien invasion movies to guess what might happen next. The creature was either going to impregnate me with its insidious offspring, kidnap me to perform horrible scientific experiments to learn more about earthling anatomy, or warn me to stop making nuclear weapons or else its fleet would utterly annihilate the planet.

Nothing good was going to come of this.

The creature didn't move, and I wondered if it was trying to communicate with me telepathically. Maybe

I was too freaked out to receive its messages. Or, I wasn't the "chosen one" with the proper mental capacities to be a telepath.

The chill of absolute terror filled my entire body, and I knew I was going to die. Amazingly, I wasn't afraid of death. Death was something I had lived with for half of my life. My only regret was how Mom and Dad were going to be devastated, having lost both of their children. Amazingly, my emotions shifted. Instead of feeling panic or dread, I felt grief. The impact of my death on Mom and Dad became the only thing on my mind at that moment.

I gave moving my limbs another try, but whatever power this monster had seized me again. The creature flinched, and its wings unfurled from behind its back and opened to full wingspan.

Its wings looked like that of a dragon or a giant bat. Shimmering gray feathers, which ruffled in the breeze, covered them. The beast turned its head upwards and flapped its wings, the tornadic winds nearly knocking me over.

It launched straight up into the air. It continued to thrash its wings until it went into a gentle glide about fifty feet above me. After completing a wide circle above, it flew towards the landfill and disappeared behind the giant mound of radioactive trash.

The trance broke, and I had full control of my body again. Instead of experiencing a complete meltdown, I sat in my car with the door open, still in shock. My face felt hot to the touch. Was I coming down with something? Maybe the alien had infected me with some extraterrestrial virus, and now I would spread it to the rest of my fellow humans, igniting a compete extinction of my race.

My eyes burned. I kept them closed for a while, as I felt like I hadn't blinked during the entire experience. When I opened my heavy lids, I knew I needed to get home before I fell asleep. All I wanted to do was hit the pillow and pass out.

The Toyota Dad had handed down to me the year before wasn't very new, but it was reliable. When I turned the ignition, it hesitated before turning over. Maybe my battery was dying. Or could the electrical delay have been connected to the flying alien?

I had the urge to call the others and tell them what had happened, but I didn't have the energy. Sleep was calling.

Was it another nightmare?

I woke up the next morning just before sunrise. That was a rarity. I always needed my alarm clock to pull me to full fight-or-flight mode, since I was a heavy sleeper. My eyes still hurt, and when I rubbed them, the searing pain made me groan in agony. I shut my eyes and left my bedroom.

With heavy feet, I stumbled across the hall into my bathroom. I didn't dare switch on the light, so I relied on the soft glow of the night light plugged in near the sink. After taking probably one of the longest pisses in all of pissing history, I glanced up at the mirror while washing my hands. I didn't recognize myself. I blinked my sore eyelids to make sure I was seeing straight.

My forehead, both cheeks, and my chin were beet red. My skin was hot to the touch. I doused my face with cold water, which only relieved the pain for a few seconds. When I looked down, I noticed both of my forearms were also sunburned.

I flicked the light switch on, and the brightness of the light struck me like an axe to the head. After flailing blindly towards the wall, I slapped the light switch down. Before I panicked, I needed to make sure I was actually awake. I gave my face a light slap, and the sharp anguish confirmed this was no dream.

Dad was probably already getting ready to walk out the door. I didn't want Mom to see me first, as she tended to think every little bump was a tumor. Every headache was an aneurysm.

I hurried down the hall into the kitchen. "Dad, can you check my face?"

"Your face?" Dad put down his briefcase and approached. He turned on the kitchen light. "Let me see."

The sudden burst of florescent light made me wince. "The light hurts my eyes."

"Were you out in the sun yesterday?" Dad asked me as he inspected my sizzling face.

"I was at Corazon Park," I replied.

Dad paused before continuing his inspection. "Did you go to the lake?"

I nodded.

"You didn't wear sunglasses?"

"No." I reached over and turned off the kitchen light. "The sunburn actually doesn't bother me as much. But my eyeballs are on fire. Hurts to even blink."

Dad sighed and stepped away. "Corazon, huh?"

I sat down, preparing myself for questioning, although Dad usually didn't grill me like Mom did. He could convey more by just standing there looking at you with his disapproving look.

"We just hung out for a little bit," I said. "I dragged everybody down there."

"Looks like you're going to miss yet another day of school." Dad put his car keys down. "You probably need to go see the optometrist. And put some aloe vera gel on your skin. We've got some in the laundry room in the cabinet."

My head hung low as I lumbered past him.

"I'll go tell your mother to call Dr. Knox and see if they can get you in right away." Dad left the kitchen to go to the master bedroom, but he stopped and swiveled around for a moment. "Your mother won't like the idea of you going back to the park."

I exhaled a shaky breath. "I know."

Dr. Knox had turned the lights down in his exam room, and I immediately felt relief. After a close examination, he turned to Mom with absolutely no expression on his wrinkled face. His bushy eyebrows raised, and he rolled his little stool away from me.

"Am I going blind?" I asked.

"No," Dr. Knox said, not catching my sarcasm. "Photokeratitis."

Mom crossed her arms. "Photo-what?"

"It's a fancy way of saying his cornea was sunburned. We see it most often in those who go skiing and forget to wear their goggles or go to the beach without proper sunglasses." Dr. Knox jotted down notes in my file. "You said you were by Corazon Lake, so that would make sense. Water reflects UV rays, so you were getting UV light from above and below."

"I bought you sunglasses in May," Mom scolded me. "Why don't you ever wear them?"

"I put them on when I'm driving," I said.

Dr. Knox said, "That's always a good idea, especially if it's polarized. Helps cut down on the glare.

You'd be amazed to learn how many car accidents occur because of sun glare. Interestingly, UV light isn't a concern inside your car, since your windshield blocks it."

Mom didn't look eager for a lecture on the dangers of UV light. "So, what does Elijah need?"

I normally would have protested her absentmindedly calling me by my brother's name, but I just wasn't in the mood.

Dr. Knox's roundish head tilted. "Elijah?"

Mom gave me an apologetic look, and her face softened. "I'm sorry," she whispered to me. She turned back to the optometrist. "What does Jonah need?"

"Nothing major, Mrs. Ashe," Dr. Knox replied as he went back to scribbling away. "I'm going to prescribe eye drops to reduce the inflammation. Just use it once a day, preferably in the morning. Shirley up front will also give you a bottle of artificial tears. Use it a couple times during the day when the pain comes back. You can take some ibuprofen or acetaminophen for the pain."

"Doesn't sound too bad," I said.

Mom didn't look too pleased. "Is he OK to go to school?"

Dr. Knox shook his head. "Not today. Keep him in a dark room for the rest of the day, no computer screens or TV." He reached over and patted my shoulder. "You might want to turn down the brightness of your phone. In fact, if you can manage, don't use your phone too much today. Wear sunglasses if you have to be out. Shirley will also give you temporary shields we give patients who get their eyes dilated, if you don't have any sunglasses for the car ride home.

"You'll be just fine in two days. At your age, you'll heal quickly." The doctor rose from his stool and left us in the exam room.

I got up from my chair, but Mom blocked my exit.

"Why did you go to Corazon?" she asked me in a low voice.

She hadn't said much in the car during the drive to see the eye doctor, but I wasn't in the mood to talk about it now. I just wanted to slather my face in more aloe gel and lay down in my bedroom with the lights off and the window shades drawn.

"Can we talk about it later?"

"Is it because it's your birthday next week?" Mom wasn't going to let this go. "Nothing good can come from going back to that park. It will just make you miserable."

Did she think my eyeballs and skin getting fried was punishment for going to the lake? That was actually a more reasonable explanation compared to the true cause of my suffering. Somehow, the winged alien was connected. I knew it had made me sick. Sunburn might be the least of my worries.

I started to panic as a horrible thought finally came

to mind. What if I was mutating? What if the alien had subjected me to some kind of radiation that was altering my DNA? My common sense woke up and temporarily shoved my paranoia away.

"I understand," I said weakly.

"Good." Mom moved aside and let me go through the doors. "I don't want to hear about you going back to that park ever again."

I should have just kept my mouth shut, but I felt like crap and I was grumpy from being so miserable. As I walked out the door, I whispered, "Calling me Elijah again isn't helping either, Mom."

CHAPTER 6

EVEN WITH MY phone's brightness all the way down, it hurt to even look at my phone to text Shannon and the others that I was OK. In my room, I had all the lights off, and just a hint of sunlight was able to penetrate my closed blinds and drapes. I had to put my sunglasses on in the dark just to be able to look at my phone.

My body craved sleep, but I was afraid of the nightmares ready to greet me the moment I dozed off. Even though I fought to stay awake, it didn't stop my imagination from running wild. I replayed my encounter with the monster over and over again. My autobiographical memory might have been uncanny, but I didn't want to forget one single detail.

In those moments between wakefulness and sleep, I kept having strange visions. They had nothing to do with the flying creature or even my brother. Vivid images of some kind of violent disaster flashed in my mind's eye. Exhaustion could play tricks on the mind. I was never a fan of disaster movies, so why were such scenes running through my brain?

I imagined twisted metal on a grassy field, flames, and sirens. Then, an unseen woman started screaming. It sounded like she was being stabbed with a kitchen knife, and then I caught what sounded like a horrific chorus of people sobbing. Although I didn't see any bodies or blood, I sensed there were dead people scattered all over the grass.

At first, I thought I was just imagining a plane crash scene from a movie I had seen a couple of years ago, but I couldn't help but think these gory images and sounds were some kind of subconscious cry for help. Maybe I was more messed up than I thought. Bring on the nut house.

Had I let things get out of control? Sitting down and talking to Ms. Kim might not be enough. I was beyond counseling. The sheer horror of realizing I might be actually losing my mind made me jump from my bed and go into the kitchen. I didn't care if the sunlight was going to feel like daggers going through my eyeballs. I needed to be reminded the outside world still existed outside my dark, twisted mind.

I went straight to the kitchen table and sat down with my eyes closed. Even with my sunglasses on, the burst of light made my head throb with agony. The sun still shone, and the sound of the mailman slamming our mailbox brought me out of my mental fog. A depressed person should never have to sit all alone with his crazy thoughts in the darkness.

Bad things might happen.

"So, you had to sit here in the dark all day?" Shannon asked.

The sun had just sunk below the horizon, so it was safe for me to pull open my window's drapes. I took off my sunglasses, and when I blinked, they didn't feel as sore as they had early that morning. Dr. Knox did say the eye was a fast healer.

"It sucked," I said as I plopped down on my bed. "Hopefully, I'll be good enough to go to school tomorrow."

Shannon twirled in my computer chair. "You keep missing school, you might not graduate." She threw me a sideways grin. "And how the hell did you get all sunburned? Dylan is the palest person I know, and he didn't even get red. We were all by the lake, and none of us got fried. So, what happened with you?"

I struggled to come up with a good excuse, but there was no fooling Shannon. She could smell any of my lies from a million light years away. Against my better judgment, I knew I had to come clean with everything that had been happening to me.

"I saw the flying creature again," I whispered.

Shannon nearly fell out of her chair. "You what? Seriously?"

"Yeah. After I dropped all of you off, I saw it flying around and followed it to my dad's warehouse. For some reason, the thing liked to fly over the landfill. Then, out of nowhere, it landed right in front of me."

Shannon sighed. "You really need to stop this. You're not funny."

I tried to give her my very best earnest face. "I'm telling you the truth. The monster stood there, right next to my car. It had to be at least seven feet tall, with arms and legs, just like you said."

She still looked unconvinced, but she asked, "What did it look like, then?"

"Its eyes were mega-bright red and they glowed. They blinded me. I couldn't even look at the thing for very long." My body began to quiver just thinking about the creature. "It had grayish skin and limbs, just like you said, but I wasn't able to see any details. The thing had huge-ass wings and feathers. I could see it, but I couldn't stare at it. Does that make any sense?"

Shannon stared into my eyes for a long time, trying to detect any trace of dishonesty. "Damn. Even with your blood shot eyes, I can tell you're telling the truth. You are serious, aren't you?"

"I am. Just look at me, Shannon. I look like toasted

ravioli."

She looked like she was going to play-slap me like she always did, but she pulled back her hand. "You think that's how you got all sunburned? And your eyes? You think the flying creature had something to do with burning your eyeballs?"

I shrugged. "I can't think of any logical explanation for what's going on."

Shannon sat silently, but I could almost hear her mind working. "So, you're toe-to-toe with this thing. Then what?"

"I couldn't move," I replied. "Not a muscle. I wanted to run, scream for help, but somehow, the monster had some kind of hold on me. It was messed up. After a few minutes, it spread its huge wings and flew away. Then I could move again. I jumped in my car, drove home, and went straight to bed. Woke up miserable and crispy."

Shannon looked absolutely freaked out. Normally, she would have felt vindicated and gloated that she had noticed how the monster had arms and legs. She glanced out at the window as if she thought the creature might come back. "Now I'm too scared to go outside. What do you think this thing is? Some kind of extraterrestrial?"

"That was my first thought," I said. "But I have to tell you something else."

"There's more?"

Even in my dim bedroom, I saw her face go pale.

"Before I even saw the alien again, I've had two nightmares about it." I clutched the edge of my bed and planted my feet on the floor. "In my dreams, I saw its red eyes. That's what makes all of this even weirder. I knew it had red, glowing eyes. When it stood right in front of me in the flesh, there they were. Red, glowing eyes. I wonder if they emitted some kind of radiation. Might explain my burns."

Shannon left my chair and sat next to me on my bed. "I know you're not making this up. This is too crazy even for you."

"I wish I was making this up," I said. "I can't tell my mom or dad. They already think I'm clinically depressed. I'd be in a straightjacket for sure if I told them everything."

"We need to tell the others," Shannon said. "Especially Brandon. He's the king of research. Let him do some digging and see if he can come up with something." She turned to my laptop. "I guess it hurts to look at the screen?"

"I tried to earlier, but I can't," I said. "Somebody around town has had to see this thing too. I mean, it's flying in circles right over the landfill. You can't tell me the four of us are the only witnesses to this monster."

Shannon left my bed and sat back on my computer chair, rolling herself towards my desk. "I can check out all those paranormal message boards too. Maybe somebody outside of St. Louis has seen something similar before. You never know."

That was a great idea, and I nodded in agreement.

"You know, if your story were to go public, nobody would ever believe you," Shannon said. "You're president of the high school science fiction club. You kind of lose some credibility there."

I had to laugh. "Yeah. Maybe if I was captain of the football team, people would take me seriously."

Because Shannon was considered the most level-headed of the group, I had her call Dylan and Brandon and fill them in on the details on a three-way call. I lay in bed while she explained everything, and I could tell they both believed her right away. Dylan admitted he too has had a nightmare or two about the flying creature, and all of this was right up Brandon's alley.

Cryptozoology was his thing, and he already had a few theories. He promised to scour the internet after he finished his honors English reading assignment and share his findings with us at school the next day.

After Shannon hung up, she got her backpack and made for my door. "I really don't want to go back out there," she said. "And there's no way I'm going to get any sleep tonight." She unzipped one of the compartments on her backpack and found her keys. "What are the odds of you being able to go to school tomorrow?"

I glanced at my laptop computer screen, and other than a dull pain, I was able to look at it at length. "Eighty percent chance I'll make it in," I replied. "I might have to wear my sunglasses in class."

"Really?" Shannon laughed. "People are going to think you're just being an ass."

"I've got a doctor's note and everything," I said. "I think I've missed two days of school all of last year. This sucks. My senior year is not off to such a great start."

The smile on Shannon's face evaporated. "Are you sure you're OK? Other than the obvious, I know you've got other stuff going on inside that brain of yours."

"Head's still above water," I answered her. "I have my moments, but I eventually snap out of it. I will probably have my annual visit to my counselor. Usually, I do it just to make my parents happy, but I'm starting to think I do need to seek some serious mental help."

Shannon shook her head at my joke. "I'm sure you're not crazy. Had we all not seen the creature last weekend, I might think differently. Ever since that night, you have been acting really strangely."

"You accuse me of being a weirdo all the time!" I protested.

"Weirder than usual," she said. "You seem more distant. And going to the park and stuff...that was a strange surprise. I'm still not convinced it was healthy for you to revisit the lake. Might have done more harm than good."

For one fleeting second, I had a flash of a revelation, but I wasn't able to hold onto it. My mind couldn't focus.

"You looked like you were going to say something," Shannon said.

"Yeah, but I forgot." I scratched my head, dumbfounded. "I think I'm sleep deprived on top of all this crap. I'm afraid to sleep."

Shannon opened my door. "You get some rest. I'm sure Brandon will have something for us tomorrow. He said he had something to do before school, so he'll catch up with us after class." She hesitated, as if she didn't want to leave. "I guess I'll see you tomorrow?"

I nodded. "Pretty sure."

She stepped out into the hallway and closed the door behind her, only to open it again and stick her head in my room. "Do you really think the creature is an alien?"

It would've been easy to just say yes. Instead, I replied, "No. I think it's much worse."

Of course, I got a lot of stares from everybody as I spent the entire day wearing sunglasses. A few teachers stopped me, and I had to explain how my corneas had been fried by the sun. None of them doubted me since my face and my arms were as red as a lobster's shell.

Time moved at a snail's pace, and I was ready for the day to be over to meet up with Brandon and the others after school. I hadn't seen him all day, as our schedules put us at the opposite ends of the school every hour, it seemed. Shannon and Dylan were already out front, letting the herd of hurrying students run to their buses and car rides home.

"How are you feeling?" Shannon asked me.

"Not too bad." I pulled down my sunglasses, and I had to squint from the sunlight. "It doesn't hurt as much today."

Dylan shook his head. "Man, you look like hell."

"You don't look so hot either," I shot back. I pointed to his messy hair, which was usually groomed neatly with extra gel for good measure. "Did you just jump out of bed and go to school like that?"

"Actually, yeah." Dylan did his best to tame his crazy hair. "I couldn't sleep too well after Shannon told me what happened to you. I haven't slept much, actually, since that night."

"You and me both," I said.

Shannon clicked her tongue. "Where is Brandon?"

GATEWAY MOTHMAN

The three of us searched the thinning crowd, and Brandon was nowhere to be found. A huge group of band kids carrying their instruments marched by, heading for their practice field. I thought Brandon wouldn't be able to contain himself after doing his research, and his absence worried me.

"Did you see him at school at all today?" I asked the others.

Dylan nodded. "We had lunch together. He hardly said a word, but he was in a hurry. Said he had to rush to the computer lab or something."

I pulled my cell phone from my backpack to send him a quick text, hoping his phone was on. Before I could even type one letter, I heard Brandon call out to us from one of the side doors. With papers in his hand, he hurried across the sidewalk. He took a moment to catch his breath.

"Sorry. I had to print this out," he said in between gasps.

"Did you find anything?" I asked.

Brandon handed the papers over to me. At the bottom of the first page was a drawing of what looked like a giant owl with beady, red eyes. I merely glanced at the headline before skimming the body of the article.

"What is it?" Shannon tried reading over my shoulder.

I read the headline out loud. "The Mothman?"

Brandon looked as serious as I'd ever seen him.

"Yeah. It's literally all right there. The first picture isn't quite right, but there's more. The stuff I found explains it all, man. The nightmares you've been having, your eyes and face getting sunburned, and the red eyes. Everything. It's definitely the Mothman."

CHAPTER 7

I READ AND reread each of the five articles Brandon had printed out and handed them out to the others after finishing each one. "I'd heard of the Mothman, but I had no idea the myth had an actual backstory."

"It all adds up," Brandon said as he pulled out a granola bar from his backpack. "The stupid printer ran out of ink, and I didn't want to wait for them to refill it, but there's way more stuff out there about it. There were so many stories and eyewitnesses out of Point Pleasant who literally saw this thing."

Dylan tapped my shoulder. "It says here one person had all kinds of burns after seeing the Mothman up close."

"Yeah, I read that." I suddenly became dizzy, so I sat down at the edge of the sidewalk. "Did you read about the Silver Bridge?" I asked him.

Shannon shuffled her papers. "I think I have that part." She passed her short stack to Dylan. "Like Brandon said, a bunch of people saw the Mothman hanging out at some old factory, and many in Point Pleasant believed the Mothman served as a bad omen. Sure enough, the Silver Bridge collapsed."

Dylan continued to read feverishly. "Forty-six people died on December 15, 1967. Tons of cars were on the bridge since it was rush hour. After the bridge collapsed, sightings of the Mothman stopped. Holy crap, look at the statue they put up in the town."

I didn't need to look at the papers anymore. "Seven feet tall with red eyes and huge wings. Yup, they got it pretty right, except its skin was a darker gray. And its wings were way bigger. The statue looks like it had butterfly wings, but from what I saw, its wings were more shaped like giant bat wings with feathers."

"Skeptics think witnesses actually saw a specific type of large crane," Dylan added.

I couldn't help but laugh at such a stupid idea. "Crane. Yeah right."

"The Mothman is a harbinger of disaster," Brandon said as he sat down next to me. "Long after the Silver Bridge, people reported seeing it just before the Twin Towers were destroyed, when the swine flu broke out in Mexico, and right before the huge tsunami in Japan in 2011."

Shannon shivered. "That is messed up."

"Is this for real?" Dylan handed Brandon the papers. "Is this really happening?"

"Just look at me," I said. "One of those papers talks about the Mothman emitting some kind of radiation. I hope I don't come down with cancer or something."

The four of us didn't say a word for a long time. Only a handful of students walked past us, heading towards the parking lot. Eventually, even some of the teachers were exiting the building and heading home.

"Practically everyone in that West Virginia town saw the Mothman," Brandon said. "If it was one or two sightings, you could say they were just seeing things. Maybe they just saw a giant crane. But there were literally hundreds of sightings, and I'm pretty sure none of us are insane. We all saw it last Sunday."

I stood up, a million thoughts tumbling in my head. "I just can't believe nobody else in town has seen it."

"It's just a matter of time," Brandon said. "If it keeps flying around the landfill, someone's bound to see it."

"Chances are, people around here have actually already seen it," Shannon said. "Maybe they're like us, afraid to say anything. I bet if you post something on the UFO Network website, other reports will follow."

Shannon was on to something.

"So, you think I should report it to the Network?" I asked her.

"Yes. Once other witnesses realize they're not

alone, they might share their own stories." Shannon looked as if she might throw up. "I just want to know I'm not crazy. That none of us are. I'd feel better knowing others have seen this thing too."

I reached into my pocket and found my car keys. "Can you guys come over to my house? I'll post it up on the UFO Network, and we can see what happens. We can read up on the Mothman in the meantime, separate what makes sense and what doesn't."

Brandon asked, "Then what?"

"I don't know," I replied. "I just need to get to the bottom of this, so I can finally get some sleep."

Everyone crowded around my computer as I entered both of my sightings on the Missouri chapter of the Collaborative UFO Network website. I tried to be as descriptive as I could without sounding hysterical. I simply stated everything I had seen without including any crazy conclusions my mind had been making. Not once did I even type the word Mothman. I did my best to be an objective observer.

"That looks pretty good," Brandon said over my right shoulder.

I read my final entry one last time before submitting and sitting back. "I guess we just wait."

"Maybe Brandon should take over and do his

thing," Shannon said.

Without second guessing Shannon's wisdom, I jumped out of my chair and let Brandon take the helm. I went to my bed and lay down. Staring at the computer screen hadn't hurt too bad, but I felt a headache coming on. At least the skin on my face wasn't burning as badly.

"Wasn't there a movie about the Mothman?" Dylan asked as he sat down on my carpeted floor, near my bed. "Or am I confusing it with *The Butterfly Effect*?"

Shannon watched Brandon continue to do his research on my laptop. "No, I think there was a movie."

"Maybe we should watch it," Dylan suggested. "Just to get a better idea of what we're dealing with."

I had no desire to watch a movie. "Movies about true events are always screwed up. Hollywood likes to change the facts for the sake of sensationalism. I have a feeling watching a movie about the Mothman is just going to piss me off."

When I closed my eyes, I couldn't stop imagining the Mothman's eyes. All I wanted was to make sense of all of this and get it behind me. I had enough to deal with. With our birthday coming up in just four days, I knew my depression was going to emerge just as it always did every year. It was going to take all of my strength to keep from sinking too deep this time around.

"Have you thought about school?" Shannon asked me.

I shook myself free from my dark thoughts. "School?"

"Yeah. College, I mean." Shannon came over and inspected my burned face. "I just wanted to talk about something normal for a change, OK? Just trying to distract myself from having a nervous breakdown."

I had thought about my future all summer to the point where I got sick of it. I was never very good at making big decisions, and that's why Mom often tried to push her influence on me. Much of it was my fault, since I let her take the wheel.

"I might take a year off," I replied. "Maybe work full-time first. It'll give me the time to make the right decision."

Dylan and Shannon exchanged surprised looks.

"Really?" Dylan looked disappointed. "I thought you might join me in Rolla. No one else I know is going there."

"It's still on the table," I said. "I guess it just depends on what I want to do with the rest of my life. I'm not ready to fully commit yet. Mom wants me to go to Mizzou, but I probably won't go there just to spite her."

Shannon slapped my foot. "Hey, your mom is pretty cool."

"She's a dictator," I said as I folded my hands

behind my head. "She bosses me around all the time. I'm going off to college just to get some breathing room."

"At least she cares about you," Shannon said with a hint of anger in her voice. "My mom doesn't care if I get a full ride to Stanford or work at McDonald's. At least your mom wants the best for you. Yeah, she's a little bossy, but that's because she gives a damn."

Shannon was right, as always.

"That's true," I said. "I'm just half-joking."

Dylan fiddled with his phone. "Richard Gere."

I dragged my legs off my bed and sat up. "What the hell are you talking about?"

"The Mothman movie," Dylan said. "Richard Gere is in it." He held up his phone. "I was reading some of the reviews. Looks like a crappy movie anyway."

We had scattered our textbooks and papers all over my bedroom floor to look like we were studying. Since it was the first week of school, none of us had much homework, but should Mom or Dad check in on us, we'd look busy. Sure enough, Mom knocked on the door before handing us two pizzas.

I immediately felt guilty for calling Mom "bossy," even though that was one of her defining personality traits. Her heart was in the right place, and like

Shannon said, at least I was lucky enough to have a mother who cared about me.

Sometimes, however, she cared a little too much.

I handed out the paper plates, and the four of us ate the still-hot pizza as we sat on the floor. Brandon chewed slowly, as if he was trying to collect his thoughts. He had left my laptop screen open, and I caught an inaccurate drawing of the Mothman. The image on the screen looked more like a dragon.

The Mothman was much more humanoid.

"I found some really messed up stuff," Brandon said after finishing his second piece. He turned to me with wide eyes. "It's all a bunch of theories, but some of it matches up with everything you've experienced."

I grabbed another slice and sat on my bed. "Like what?"

Brandon replied, "Many of the people in Point Pleasant believe the Mothman is part of an Indian curse. Some think it's literally a creature from another dimension. Others say it's some kind of angel. One thing is for sure, though: it seems to always show up right before something tragic happens."

"Sounds like the stuff you printed out at school," Shannon said.

"The movie Dylan was talking about was actually based on a book," Brandon continued. "The author was in Point Pleasant and investigated all the weird stuff going on there. Other than the obvious Mothman sightings, there were crazy UFOs reported by the townspeople. Point Pleasant was where people first saw the Men in Black."

I did my best to follow what Brandon was saying, but his findings were getting more and more farfetched. "Men in Black? Are you serious? Like Will Smith?"

"Government agents," Brandon replied. "But it gets even weirder. We already know that some of the folks who saw the Mothman face-to-face also had their eyes literally burned, just like you. Another witness even had blood come out of her ears. Something about being exposed to ultraviolet rays."

My stomach threatened to weaken, making me regret stuffing four slices of pizza down my throat. Dylan and Shannon stared at me, in awe of Brandon's revelation. I felt vindicated, yet terrified at the same time.

"I'm not done," Brandon whispered in a creepy voice. "There was a journalist in Point Pleasant who had nightmares about people drowning. Her prophesy came true when the Silver Bridge collapsed."

Dylan dropped his pizza on his plate. "I've been having nightmares too, but it's just of people running and screaming. It was terrifying enough to wake me up."

"Me too," Shannon said. "Just one nightmare, actually. The night we saw it, I dreamed about being on top of a mountain, and suddenly, it started to cave in. It was so real, I woke up screaming."

We turned to Brandon, but he shook his head.

"I don't remember my dreams," Brandon said.

"I didn't used to remember mine either, Brandon, so you're lucky." I got up and started to pace beside my bed. "Maybe something bad is going to happen here."

Shannon said, "That's what I was thinking."

"Why is it flying around the landfill?" Dylan asked Brandon. "Does it actually like the stench?"

Brandon said, "In Point Pleasant, the Mothman was sighted a bunch of times at some abandoned TNT plant, but I have no idea if a TNT plant smells bad. Can't stink nearly as bad as the landfill, though."

"A TNT plant might have some toxic crap left over," I said. "The landfill has all the radioactive stuff from the Philadelphia Experiment."

Shannon laughed at me. "Manhattan Project, dummy. You're getting your secret government projects mixed up."

"So now what?" Dylan asked nobody in particular. "Should we tell somebody?"

Brandon went back to my laptop and scrolled through a few pages. "Nobody's posted anything else on the UFO Network."

Even though my blood ran cold every time I thought about the Mothman standing in front of me, a part of me wanted to go out and keep an eye on the skies. I didn't want to see it again, but deep down, I felt a need to go to the landfill in the hopes of having another sighting. This time, I'd prefer to see it from a distance. The others would never go for it, and I knew I'd end up chickening out anyway.

"Maybe we should pay more attention to our dreams," I said.

Shannon nodded. "I could keep a notebook on my nightstand and write stuff down before I forget."

"That's a good idea." I had lost my appetite and put my half-eaten pizza slice on my desk. "We should all do it, just in case. Maybe the Mothman is here to warn us. I think that's what it was doing in Point Pleasant, but the people didn't listen."

Shannon shivered again. "I'd feel better if other people came forward about seeing it."

I pointed a thumb at my laptop. "Let's keep an eye on the website. If anybody else posts something about the Mothman, we'll reach out to each other. I guess we'll just have to figure out why the Mothman is here."

"It's obvious to me," Brandon said. "Something huge is going to happen, some kind of disaster. And a lot of people are literally going to die."

Usually, I poked fun at Brandon's crazy declarations about the impending apocalypse, but not this time.

CHAPTER 8

AT FIRST, KEEPING a dream journal next to my bed sounded like a good idea, but I wasn't sure how disciplined I would be. I had never been good at keeping any kind of journal, even for ninth grade language arts when we were required to write in one every day. I was satisfied with my ability to mull over my life's events in my head, and I saw no need to write them down. Journaling was unnecessary.

The rest of the first week of school went by without incident. My eyes had healed, and other than some peeling of dead skin, the burns on my face and arms went away pretty quickly. Shannon and Dylan didn't have any nightmares either, and Brandon continued to sleep soundly after checking all the various UFO and crypto message boards and websites for even a hint of somebody else in the St. Louis area witnessing the Mothman flying over town.

GATEWAY MOTHMAN

After meeting with the gang and a few other members of our school's science fiction club at Sella's Pizza on Friday evening, I was too exhausted to do anything else. I went straight home, checked a few websites, and went to bed.

Before falling asleep, I glanced at the open notebook and pen on my nightstand. I vowed to write down every detail of any dream I would have, even if it seemed mundane and irrelevant to the Mothman.

I drifted off easily and forced myself to wake up after my first dream. As always, I had no idea what time it was. I could've dozed off for an hour or it might have been eight the next morning. Using the harsh light from my phone, I jotted down everything I could remember.

It was still too dark to read what I had written, and I was too tired to even try. My dream had been very ordinary. I was at school, going through the motions of sitting in class. The TV in the corner of the room kept flashing a baseball score. The Cardinals had beaten the Reds 14-2. My conscious mind pulled me out of my dream and allowed me to write it all down.

I checked the time on my phone, and it wasn't even eleven o'clock yet. In fact, I could see a flicker of light coming from under my door. Mom was our resident insomniac, and she was probably watching some sentimental show on the Lifetime Channel or an infomercial.

With some effort, I relaxed my mind and fell asleep again.

All kinds of debris covered the street. Pieces of insulation, large sections of siding and wood, and I even noticed what remained of a barbecue grill laying on its side. The sky above me swirled. At first, the clouds were dark gray, but everything became the color of blood.

For a split second, my conscious mind awoke to notice the red sky; this had to be my third or fourth dream with this same imagery. Someone's car alarm continued to blare, and sirens wailed from afar.

I hurried down the sidewalk, eager to take shelter. The storm seemed to be moving away from my position, but I couldn't shake the feeling I wasn't safe yet. Thunder rumbled, and lightning struck a nearby tree. The sonic boom rattled my ears, and I even checked to make sure I wasn't bleeding.

My foot caught on something, which sent me headfirst into the muddy earth. I tasted dirt, and my knees throbbed. When I got back on my feet, I bent down to tie my unraveled shoelace. That's when my foot nudged a twisted corpse.

I nearly tripped over my own feet, and it took me several moments to catch my breath. The person's legs lay at unnatural angles, but his face, thankfully, was turned away from me. I knew I needed to just get out of there before another storm hit, but I couldn't help it. I had to know who had died.

After seeing so many zombie flicks, I stepped around the body carefully, as if it might awaken and try to devour me. I tapped the poor guy's shoulder with my foot, and sure enough, he was permanently dead.

I crouched to get a closer look, as the man's face was covered with mud. His eyes remained closed, which was a relief, but I couldn't tell who it was. I needed to wipe the crud off of his face to identify him, but there was no way I was going to touch him.

A harsh, cold wind turned my blood into ice, and it magically blew the dirt off of the man's face. When his eyelids opened, I screamed so loud, it drowned out the approaching sirens.

I shrieked at my own face looking up at me with lifeless eyes.

Now I knew how Luke Skywalker felt when he had his own crazy hallucination on Dagobah in *The Empire Strikes Back*. I backed away and tripped over another body. This one looked female, but her face was too mangled to tell who she was. Her hair was silver, and she still clutched a rosary in her stiff hands.

More thunder rolled in from the red sky. I needed to find some shelter right away, but the ground became littered with more and more bodies, spread out as far as I could see. The mud became saturated with blood, and my conscious mind made a feeble attempt to remind me this was just a nightmare.

Taking careful steps around the scattered, dead bodies all around me, I went back to the dead version of me. I dropped to my knees, and I couldn't help but stare at my own face. After a few moments, I realized there was some kind of sticker on his shirt. I wiped away the soot, and it was one of those "HELLO My Name Is" nametags.

In handwriting that looked like that of a child, it said, "ELIJAH."

I grabbed my brother by his shirt and shook him, trying to wake him up. But he was lifeless. He had died in the storm that had torn through the area. With some reluctance, I let Elijah's body fall back to the blood-soaked earth.

"I'm so sorry," I said to him. "I would trade places with you, if I could."

Elijah's brown eyes became bright red. The light coming from them blinded me. His mouth moved, but I was jolted awake before I could hear what my dead brother was trying to tell me.

My pillow was soaked with sweat when I nearly threw myself off my bed and forced myself to wake up. The nightmare was fresh in my mind, so I turned on my phone and scribbled in the notebook.

I wrote everything down, not leaving one detail out.

Even as I sat on my bed writing, I could still smell the wet earth lingering in my nostrils. The realness of my dream told me these visions were not just my subconscious trying to work things out.

My words flowed onto the paper, and I filled up three full pages when I finished. I left my bed, pulled off my t-shirt, and used it as a towel to wipe the sweat off the rest of my body. It would be useless to try to get anymore sleep. I looked at my phone, and I couldn't believe it was a minute past five in the morning. My dream felt like only five, ten minutes at the most, had passed.

I went to my window and opened the blinds. It still looked like nighttime outside. Part of me wanted to get back to bed and try to catch more sleep, but I went to my computer instead.

The first website I went to was a well-known UFO reporting website, although it didn't carry the same kind of legitimacy as the UFO Network. When I went through the list of the most recent sightings, I found one from the St. Louis area. I stared at the post's title for a long time.

"Flying Man in St. Louis"

I took a deep breath before clicking the link to the

post.

"Just this evening, me and my friends were out near the old Northland Plaza Mall, and we saw what we first thought had to be a mutant vulture. Its wingspan was at least six feet long. We snapped pictures with our phones, but none of them came out. It flew over the mall until it took off to the southwest towards Monument High School. People waiting at the bus stop saw it too. We hope others have seen this thing. I will get a good camera and see if we can catch a decent picture of it."

I read the entry three times, and I almost called Shannon until I realized how early it was. These reports were done anonymously, so there was no way for me to reach out to the person who had posted it. But if other people had seen the Mothman, then maybe they'd come forward too.

For the first time this week, I didn't feel so crazy.

Dylan stretched his legs in the passenger seat next to me. "I think I've only sat shotgun four times since your parents got you this car. I guess you have to be the gentleman and let Shannon sit up here."

I shrugged my shoulders. "I guess. I never thought of it that way. She just always claims that spot. You know how she is."

Brandon remained in the back seat, scrolling through something on his phone. "There hasn't been another post since this morning, but that doesn't mean anything. This site is pretty barebones, so I bet not too many people know about it. Nothing yet on the Network site, though."

"Maybe give it a rest for an hour or two," I said. "You can check both sites after we pick up Shannon."

The hospital was just off of the Rock Road. I turned into the shopping center to cut through their parking lot. For a Saturday afternoon, the place was dead. Not too many shoppers out today, and it looked like the Bread Café was the busiest business in the strip.

"I hate going to the hospital," Brandon whined.

"Me too," Dylan said. "I think it's the smell. It reeks of antiseptic and bananas."

Our school required fifty hours of volunteer service for graduation. Brandon was an Eagle Scout, so he hit his goal freshman year. Dylan had worked for the Bridgetown Athletic Association, helping to maintain the ballpark grounds and concession stands. My contribution to society was a mishmash of stuff. I had volunteered at the Special Olympics every May since ninth grade, I worked at two local food pantries with Mom last year, and I helped out at the hospital's thrift store. I only needed a measly four hours to hit my goal, but Shannon had procrastinated. Now she had to get all fifty hours in one year, so she worked in patient transport at the hospital.

"It's probably because a lot of the people at the hospital are sick or dying," I said. "Just the thought of it does feel creepy, but Shannon's not working in the morgue or anything. She gets to wheel patients around, which isn't too bad."

I had texted Shannon about finding the Mothman post online, but she was too busy at the hospital to give me much of a reply. She had asked if I could pick her up when she was done volunteering to talk about it. Shannon was probably relieved like the rest of us that we weren't alone anymore. Others had seen the Mothman too. In some ways, it called for a celebration.

"Maybe the person who posted the sighting will be somewhere around here today," Brandon said. "The poster mentioned having friends who saw the Mothman too. We should hang around and meet the poster; share our story with them and see if it all matches up."

Brandon often said the first thing to pop in his mind, so he usually came up with the craziest, most off the wall ideas. We had gotten used to just laughing at him whenever he came up with one of his schemes. But lately, he'd been on a roll.

"We should," I said, trying to hide my enthusiasm. "Great idea, Brandon."

"Really?" Brandon leaned forward.

Dylan gave Brandon's curly hair a playful tussle. "Even a blind squirrel finds a nut once in a while."

We only had to wait inside my car at the front entrance for five minutes until Shannon hurried through the open doors. She wore a maroon, collared shirt, and her badge dangled from one of the collars. Shannon stopped at the passenger side, throwing Dylan a "get out of my seat or I'm going to kick your ass" look.

"Fine!" Dylan swung the door open and got out, taking his usual place next to Brandon in the rear seat. "There you go, Your Highness."

Shannon flashed me a quick smile as she sat down and shut the door. She passed me a piece of paper. "It's about the Piasa bird."

I took the article and glanced at it. "But what I saw...what we saw...wasn't a giant bird."

"That's not the point," Shannon said. "Maybe the Mothman and the legend of the Piasa bird are somehow connected."

Brandon was already furiously looking it up on his phone.

"What's a pizza bird?" Dylan asked.

"It's Piasa, not pizza." Shannon turned to face him. "And it's an old Native American legend from the Alton area. French explorers entering Cahokian territory discovered a massive painting of a winged monster on one of the cliffs in Alton."

The article was short, but Shannon was onto something.

I handed the paper to Dylan. "The Indians said this Piasa bird actually attacked people. Swooped down and ate them. A chief and his bravest warriors hunted it down in a cave and killed it."

Shannon said, "The huge painting either celebrated their victory, or it served as a warning to others. It's interesting how something like this came from just the other side of the river, don't you think?"

I started the engine. "Makes you wonder, that's for sure."

"Did you want to go to Alton to see the painting?" Shannon asked.

"It's still up?" Dylan handed the paper to Brandon.

Brandon didn't bother reading it. "The original painting is literally gone. When they were building the road, they blasted the cliff. So, they had to recreate it. It's still freaky looking, though."

"Actually, Brandon had a great idea," I said. "If the person who posted is going to be hanging out near the old mall with a camera, maybe we could go there too. We could share our story."

Shannon pointed a finger at me. "You mean your story."

"No. I'm not ready to talk about what happened

with me," I said. "My parents are already thinking I'm going to lose my mind like I usually do this time of year. I keep telling them I'm OK, but they're not buying it."

"But you're not OK," Shannon said.

I opened my mouth to argue, but I decided against it. "I think considering what's happened to me this past week, I'm handling everything like a champ."

"Hey guys," Brandon said in a high-pitched squeal. "There's been a new report on the Network."

My breath became caught in my throat. "Read it!"

"It was just posted a minute ago." Brandon brought his phone closer to his face. "It says the reporter spotted a winged object flying overhead in Well Springs in St. Charles County. It circled above the park before disappearing into the clouds. Says it's too big to be a bird."

I had never been to that part of Well Springs, and I wasn't too familiar with what was on the west side of the Missouri River. "That's incredible. Two other sightings. Maybe more will pour in. Interesting how they're seeing the Mothman in St. Charles now, though."

Dylan got out of his seat and poked his long face through the front seats. "Well Springs Park. You ever been there?"

"Nope. I don't even know where it is," I replied.

"My science class took a field trip there sophomore

year," Dylan said. "The park has this giant mound with a long stairway you can walk up. I think it's the highest point in all of St. Charles County."

"A mound? Like the Cahokia Mounds?" Shannon's eyes widened. "Is the mound in Well Springs an ancient Indian burial mound?"

"No." Dylan paused before saying, "It's some kind of protective cover housing the radioactive waste. And they used to manufacture TNT there too."

All four of us let out heavy sighs of disbelief. The dots were connecting too well.

"Whatever the Mothman is, it seems drawn to toxic waste," I said. "TNT plants, landfills, radioactive garbage."

The four of us remained lost in our own thoughts until Shannon said, "Let's go to Well Springs first, and then come back here to see if anyone is staking out the old mall with a camera."

I put the car in drive. "OK Brandon, pull up your GPS and get us to Well Springs."

CHAPTER 9

I HADN'T VENTURED over the bridge into St. Charles County very much, and it was foreign territory to many of us on the eastern side of the Missouri River Bridge. I expected to see nothing but farmland out here, but it looked identical to the suburbs in my part of St. Louis. In fact, the houses off the highway looked newer and nicer than my neck of the woods.

Brandon gave me directions from the backseat, and it took only another fifteen minutes of driving to reach Well Springs after crossing the bridge. I took another smaller highway, and that's when it got pretty rural. Once in a while, we'd spot a ginormous house on top of a hill, but the houses out here were much more spread out compared to our town.

We finally turned into Well Springs Conservation Park. The road narrowed and winded sharply until I turned into a nearly empty parking lot. A big white industrial building sat at the end of the paved area, so we parked near a white van and a silver sedan up front.

"We should be able to find the steps up the mound from here," Brandon said, still staring at his phone.

Dylan pointed to the building. "There's a museum inside of there."

I got out of my car first, and the others followed. The place was like a ghost town. Even though it was a really nice Saturday afternoon, the only sounds were the birds chirping and our footsteps smacking against the asphalt lot. I expected people to be out and walking along the trail cutting through there.

"Where is everybody?" Shannon asked no one in particular, as if she was reading my mind.

The top of the huge mound peeked over the top of the industrial building. Brandon pointed to a narrow, paved path, so without questioning his navigation, we took it. I was mesmerized by the size of the huge mountain of rock. We found the hiking trail and turned left until we found the foot of the steps leading all the way to the top of the giant mound.

"Holy crap that's a lot of steps," Brandon complained.

I grabbed onto the metal railing and took the first step. "Here we go!"

The steps' tread was made of gravel, and it took me two strides to advance each step. Only Dylan and his long legs could do it in one stride. Brandon lagged behind, and he only stopped twice to catch his breath. We all stopped with him, taking in the view as we let the burning in our lungs dissipate.

"Seventy-five feet high," Dylan said between gasps.

Rather than waste my oxygen with replying to his useless factoid, I nodded and continued to lead the way to the very top. The steps gave way to a simple gravel hill, which was a little bit easier to traverse. Once I reached the flat platform, I wanted to throw my hands up in the air in some kind of victory dance. Of course, when Brandon caught up, that's exactly what he did.

"Wow. This is pretty amazing." Shannon stared out in all directions, her mouth as wide open as her eyes. "I can see everything from up here."

It amazed me how a place so awesome was only thirty minutes from my house, yet I had never visited it. "We're currently standing on a bajillion tons of nuclear waste?"

Brandon collapsed onto one of the benches. He scrolled through his phone and said, "Forty-five acres of uranium."

Shannon went to a large memorial plaque. Her fingers ran over the embossed words as she read to herself. "This mound is supposed to contain all the radioactive material for a thousand years."

"Then what?" Brandon asked.

"Who cares." I plopped down next to Brandon. "We'll all be dead by then."

Dylan pointed to the walkway. "Looks like we've got some tourists coming up."

My legs still hurt, but I got up and tried to loosen them up. "If the Mothman is flying anywhere in the region, no doubt you'd see it from up here. Maybe we should hang out here until dark."

"You think the Mothman only comes out at night?" Shannon asked me.

"Seems like it," I replied. It would be another six hours until the sun went down. "Don't waste your phone's battery. If the Mothman makes another appearance, we need to try to get pics or video of it."

Dylan hurried over to me and tugged my arm. "Those aren't tourists."

We squinted into the distance until we knew Dylan was right. Two men in navy-blue suits and ties made their way up towards us. The one on the right had neatly combed jet-black hair, but the guy on the left wore a gray fedora hat. They both also wore sunglasses and looked like old school gangsters. Neither one spoke a word as they marched up the walkway at a steady clip.

"Who do you think they are?" Brandon asked.

Dylan speculated, "Maybe they're with the newspaper?"

"They look a little too professional to be with the

paper," Shannon said as she squinted her eagle eyes at the strangers. "They look like something out of an old movie with the way they're dressed."

I pushed everyone back. "Let's not stand here gawking at them when they get here. That'll look suspicious."

"I doubt they're here to snap pictures of birds," Brandon said is a low voice.

"We'll find out in a couple minutes." I jogged back to the bench. "Let's not say anything about the Mothman," I said to the others. "Just act innocent until we find out who they are and why they're here."

Dylan and Shannon stood next to each other, pretending to stare out into the distance as if enjoying the tremendous view. They gawked at each other before Dylan asked, "Anybody else hearing static? Or have I completely lost my mind?"

Had Dylan not said anything, I would have just assumed I was simply so stressed out and nervous, which made my head pound from the increase in adrenaline and blood pressure. The birds stopped chirping, the wind stopped blowing, and yes, the sound of static filled my ears to the point where I thought I had gone batshit crazy.

"I hear it too," I replied under my breath.

By the looks on Brandon and Shannon's faces, they could hear the static as well.

"Good afternoon," the man wearing the fedora said to us as he reached the platform.

I wanted to return the greeting, but I simply nodded my head. Brandon went back to staring at his phone, while Shannon and Dylan returned to staring out into the view of all of St. Charles County. The sound of static intensified as the two men strolled casually towards me. I did my best to not stare at them, and I fought the urge to get up from the bench and run down the path. The one on my right without the hat got to me first.

He bent over me and said, "It's a beautiful day."

The man's sunglasses completely hid his eyes, and I found it hard to look up into the pitch-black lenses. "Yeah." Talking about the weather seemed like a casual thing to bring up. "It's pretty hot. But other than that, it is a beautiful day."

"See anything interesting?" he asked me.

The man stood way too close, but I resisted the instinct to scoot away. "The view is amazing. This is the highest point in all of St. Charles County. I was hoping to see the Arch from up here."

"Arch?" The stranger pulled out a small notepad and pen from his jacket pocket. "You saw an arch up here?"

I was too creeped out to reply, and Brandon must

have sensed this. He made his way over to me with slow, deliberate footsteps. "The Gateway Arch. We thought we'd be high enough to see it from here, but we couldn't," Brandon explained.

After scribbling something, the man turned around to approach Shannon and Dylan. "Did you see anything interesting?"

Shannon's tight mouth opened just wide enough to ask, "Who are you guys?"

The man with the fedora took a step towards her. "We are with an organization called UFOIL. The UFO Investigators League."

Dylan kept his arms crossed. "You want to know if we've seen a UFO from up here?"

"Yes," the Hat Man replied. "We investigate UFO sightings all over the country."

Shannon wasn't buying it. "Where are you from?"

The man with black hair replied, "UFOIL."

"No, I mean, where." Shannon put her hands on her hips. "What city?"

"Chicago." The man slid his notebook and pen back into his pocket. "We heard of several reports of UFOs being reported in the area."

The four of us exchanged nervous glances, and the others turned to me to speak for the group. Part of me wanted to bring up the Mothman. I needed to talk about how we first saw it flying around Northland Plaza. I so badly had to talk about how I've not only seen it flying near the landfill, but how I actually stood not less than five feet in front of the winged beast. My mind raced to find the right words, but I wrestled with giving ourselves away.

"We haven't seen any UFOs, if that's what you're asking." I stood up, and I was immediately hit with a dizzy spell. "I saw a family of deer near the parking lot, though."

The Hat Man swiveled around to face me. He was silent for a long time before finally saying, "Thank you for your time. Have a good day."

He led his fellow creepy buddy back down the pathway. They made their way down the tall mound, their rapid steps in sync until they disappeared over the hill. The interference in my head faded.

I led Dylan and Shannon down the gravel sidewalk, careful not to give ourselves away. The two guys had reached the portion where the sloping trail became steps again. They had parked their car right next to mine.

"That was creepy," Brandon said as he joined the rest of us watching the men get inside what looked like an antique black car. "And the static sound is gone."

Brandon was right. I no longer heard static, and the chirping of birds and whooshing of wind returned. My head stopped throbbing too. Only when the black car exited the parking lot did we finally let our guard down.

"What was all that about?" Dylan asked the group.

Shannon shook her head. "UFO Investigation League my ass!"

"One thing's for sure," I said as I took one last look out into the vastness of trees surrounding us. There wouldn't be a Mothman sighting up here today, and I just wanted to get the hell out of there.

Brandon was the first to head for the stairs. "What's that?"

I motioned for him to lead us back down the mound of radioactive waste. "The Men in Black actually wear blue."

CHAPTER 10

THE FOUR OF us hardly said a word after the Men in Black left, and we unanimously decided to not hang around the radioactive mound until dark. If the Mothman was going to fly around the Well Springs area tonight, we were going to miss its appearance. We had had enough weird, and actually seeing the flying monster would have been too much to take. No one spoke until we were a good fifteen minutes into our drive home and we hit the bridge over the Missouri River.

"I know I'm not crazy," Shannon finally said. "But we need to talk about the weird buzzing in our heads the whole time we talked to the Men in Black."

As always, Dylan popped his head forward between the front seats. "Right. I heard loud static in my head, and you all said you heard it too. The closer those two guys got to us, the louder the static got. But it wasn't just the buzzing that had messed me up. There was something else…"

The four of us knew what Dylan was talking about, but none of us wanted to admit it.

I decided to be the first to confess. "I almost talked about the Mothman. I mean, I actually wanted to tell them about it. I wanted to tell them everything."

"I literally had to bite my tongue," Brandon said. "It took all I had to keep my mouth shut. And did anyone else feel tired? The whole time they were here, I felt like I was short of breath."

Dylan nodded. "Yeah. I did feel…drained. Between the buzzing and the tiredness, I thought I just might pass out."

Shannon rolled down the window to let the August breeze hit her face. "It was messed up. It's like they had the power to weaken our will and control our minds. I felt it too. I had to fight it."

"None of us told them anything," I said. "At least we know we can resist whatever mind-bending power they've got."

Brandon said, "So not only do the Men in Black wear blue, but they have the power to make you talk. You think they have a memory wiping neuralyzer-thing like they did in the movie?"

"I wouldn't doubt it," Dylan whispered.

I said, "They were nothing like Will Smith and Tommy Lee Jones. The MIB were heroes, protectors of Earth. The last line of defense against the bad guys.

In reality, the Men in Black are the bad guys."

"Is UFOIL even a real organization?" Shannon asked.

Brandon was already on his phone. "They shut down years ago. I doubt they were from Chicago too. They literally had no idea what the Arch was."

Dylan asked the group, "So what's the plan now?"

"I get the feeling we haven't seen the last of the Men in Black," Shannon replied. "We all need to make sure to keep our guard up and fight whatever power they have. We don't talk about UFOs, the Mothman, or anything if those two guys show up at our doors."

While still surfing on his phone, Brandon said, "Hey, tomorrow's Jonah's birthday. What are your plans?"

Just like every year, Mom and Dad would take me out to dinner at the place of my choosing. Last year was Italian, but I had been thinking barbecue for my eighteenth birthday.

"Same thing we do every year. My parents will take me out to dinner. We keep it pretty low key."

They knew this was a particularly rough birthday for me. Every year, they offered to come over and help celebrate, but it took all of my energy to put on a smile for my parents. I'm pretty sure it was an exhausting effort for them too. Maybe since I was technically becoming an adult, we all thought maybe it would have been easier, but we were wrong. It was even tougher. I felt I was now really leaving Elijah behind for good. I was now a man, but he would always be a little nine-year-old boy.

"I'll keep an eye on the Network website to see if there are any others reporting Mothman sightings," Brandon said. "If anything new pops up, I'll let you know."

Dylan said, "Maybe this whole thing will just blow over."

Shannon threw him an annoyed look. "Wishful thinking."

More than wanting my birthday to pass quickly, I hoped to never see those giant, red, glowing eyes—big as baseballs—ever again. That was my birthday wish. I wished to never come face to face with the Mothman for the rest of my life. But like Shannon said, it was wishful thinking.

"I have to do another four hours at the hospital," Shannon said. "But I'll check in with you guys after."

"I've got a church thing tomorrow." Dylan leaned back in his seat. "But I can meet any time after dinner for a little bit. Maybe if you're feeling up to it, we can check out the mall like we originally talked about."

Brandon chimed in, "I can meet any time after two."

At first, I was going to tell them I was probably just going to go to bed early after my birthday dinner, but hanging out with friends would be the healthy thing to do tomorrow. "We usually do a lunch-dinner thing anyway, so yeah, if you guys can make it, let's stakeout the mall."

Shannon playfully slapped my shoulder, as usual. "What a great way to spend your birthday. Mothman hunting!"

"I still hope all of this stuff just disappears," Dylan said. "I want the world to be normal again."

"It's going to get worse," I said. "I have a feeling it's going to get even weirder around here."

The sky was a vivid blue, with only wispy, feathery clouds obscuring an otherwise perfectly clear day. In the middle of the dancing branches of the trees out in the distance, two piercing red glowing eyes stared back at me. My shoes sank into wet earth, and when I looked down, I noticed I was standing at the edge of a river.

Instead of water, it flowed with blood. It crashed against the rocks, staining them red. As always, my conscious mind stirred once again as a reminder that this was just another nightmare. There was something else in the water, so I stepped towards it, nearly getting my shoes soiled. The blood river flowed slowly, as if it had suddenly thickened. A long bone broke the surface, followed by a skull. Thousands of human remains bubbled up to the top. My jaws opened wide to scream, but nothing came out.

The ground shook, and the winds picked up. Ominous storm clouds invaded the once gorgeous sky, swirling until they formed a sinister vortex near the trees. There was no shelter anywhere for me to take cover, so I retreated away from the tornado.

I stumbled several times, losing my balance each time the earth rumbled. My mind kept repeating the same words over and over again, "this is just a nightmare; this isn't real." Then the ground felt as if it was going to rip open and swallow me whole. I stumbled again, slamming my face into the damp grass. The pain was real. This was not just a normal nightmare.

"You're right."

Elijah's voice echoed all around me. It seemed to come from the sky, as if it was God's thunderous voice about to tell me the end of the world was coming. The earthquake stopped long enough for me to regain my footing, and when I straightened up, Elijah stood directly in front of me.

When he spoke again, he sounded somewhat normal. With every syllable that came out of his ghostly mouth, the sound of crystals spilling into a glass trailed softly. "This is not just a dream," he said.

Behind me, the tornado continued to churn, but it made no sound. The only thing I could hear was Elijah. I reached out to touch him, and my hand pressed against his shoulder. It was like looking at my own reflection in the mirror. His hair wasn't longer or shorter than mine, and he wore a t-shirt and jeans just like me. I had always wondered, had he lived, if he would have rebelled against Mom wanting us to be identical in every way by dying his hair blond or getting a nose ring.

My voice returned. "Is it really you?"

He nodded. "The distance between the living and the dead is both miniscule and a billion miles long. It's easier when you're sleeping."

"Easier for me to what?"

Elijah grinned. "To have visions."

I glanced up at the apocalypse closing in on me. "What does all this mean?"

"You will figure it out." Elijah became translucent. "I can't spell it out for you."

Without having to look up, I knew the Mothman was up in the sky. Reluctantly, I turned upwards. The winged beast circled high above me, its gray bat wings flapping only occasionally. It flew with a grace that reminded me of how hawks would freely glide over their prey. Although I couldn't see the Mothman's face, his fiery red eyes seemed to be fixed on me.

"If you can't spell it out for me, can you at least give me a hint?"

Elijah cracked a mischievous smirk. "The Cardinals beat the Reds 14-2."

"What the hell does that mean?" I stole a quick glance upwards, and the Mothman was hovering closer to the ground. I kept thinking he was going to dive-bomb me at any moment. "I don't understand any of this."

"He will need you," Elijah said.

I shot back, "Who will need me?"

I could see right through his body. When I reached out to touch Elijah again, my hand went right through his apparition. As his image faded, the roaring of the tornado returned, and the burst of wind knocked me off my feet.

My body crashed into the ground, and I woke up on the floor of my bedroom.

Just like we had done the last several years, we hopped into the SUV for my birthday dinner. Two o'clock might not have been dinnertime, but we usually stuffed ourselves enough during the day to skip dinner at home.

I told Dad I wanted to go to the best barbecue place he knew. After thinking about it for a moment, we headed east on the highway towards the city. Mom was uncharacteristically quiet, but I understood why. Our birthday was always a subdued occasion. After twenty minutes, I could see the Gateway Arch in the distance.

Pop's Smokehouse was a St. Louis treasure. It was far from fancy, but the moment we stepped out of the car, I could smell the Memphis barbecue in the air. It was busy, as usual, but we were able to get a table. Our food came out quickly, and we were about halfway through our meal when Mom accidentally called me Elijah again. I normally ignored it, but something compelled me to say something this time.

Maybe it was because I was taking this birthday especially hard. Or maybe it was from a lack of sleep. The stress of everything had taken its toll on me. I immediately regretted it the moment I said, "Please, Mom. Stop calling me by my brother's name."

She and Dad exchanged nervous looks.

"I'm sorry," she said as she wiped her hands with a napkin.

I should have just stopped right there and accepted her apology. "You've been doing it a lot lately."

Once again, she glanced at Dad as if the two shared a dirty secret.

"I think this year is especially difficult," Dad said. "For all of us."

The three of us sat quietly for several moments until I opened my big mouth again. "And why is it especially difficult this year?"

"It's tough every year," he replied. "But you're eighteen now. A man."

Mom closed her eyes, and her voice was unusually

soft. "I can't help but think about my two boys becoming men." She reached over and caressed my face. "I'm sorry, Jonah."

My head felt as if a knife had pierced my forehead. "I know you're sorry. But can you please stop calling me Elijah? It hurts every time you do it. I know you're not doing it on purpose. It's just…"

Without warning, my mouth froze, unable to move. My tongue swelled. The room shook, as if a massive earthquake was going to tear the restaurant apart. From the look on my parents' faces, however, I was the only one experiencing the violent shaking. Was my food poisoned?

Dad called out to me, but I couldn't hear him. Mom moved to grab me by the shoulder. The room spun so fast, I leaned back against my seat for support. My body slumped and slid against the wooden booth until I laid down on the bench, staring up at the gyrating ceiling. All the ductwork and stuff up there had been painted black, and two red fireballs materialized out of all the blackness. The orbs grew larger and larger with every second until I had completely lost my sight.

Dad's panicked face was the last thing I saw before I blacked out.

CHAPTER 11

"**I DON'T NEED** to go to the hospital." My head rattled from the jackhammering inside my brain, and I just wanted to lie down in the back seat. But I had to convince them I was OK and another trip to the ER was unnecessary. "I'm fine. It'll be just a big waste of time and money."

Mom swiveled from the passenger seat. "You keep passing out. What if you have a tumor?"

I was going to quote *Kindergarten Cop*, but I knew it would've just set her off. "They're just going to say I'm stressed out and dehydrated before sending me home with a big bill."

It was Dad's turn to state their case. "First at school, and now at Pop's. We have to find out if there's something going on. It's probably nothing serious, but we have to make sure."

It hadn't been easy keeping everything a secret

from them, and it was making me tired having to lie to them so much. Maybe if I were to give them some answers, they'd back off. I had to let them in just a little bit, but there was no way I was going to tell them everything.

"As our eighteenth birthday got closer, I started having nightmares about Elijah."

Mom and Dad turned to each other for a moment, as if they had known my secret all this time.

"What kind of nightmares?" Mom asked.

I had to be careful to leave all the apocalyptic and Mothman stuff out of it. "I keep seeing him as if he's aged like me. He talks to me as if he's alive. It's messed up."

Dad asked, "What does he say?"

"He keeps telling me he's going to continue to show up in my dreams." That was a half-truth. "But he doesn't actually say much. It's just this feeling I get when I see him."

Mom reached out, and I took her hand. "How do you feel when you see him?"

"Like something bad is going to happen. Something awful. In one nightmare, a huge tornado came from the sky and destroyed everything."

Mom said in a soft voice, "You bottle everything up, Jonah. You can't keep all of this locked inside of you. It's starting to affect your health."

"I know." I hope I hadn't given away too much,

but I knew what was coming next.

"You need to talk to someone," Mom said. "We talked about it before, but I think we need to see if Ms. Kim is able to see you tomorrow after school."

Dad nodded. "Talking to her always did you some good. It's been a long time."

This was a descent compromise. "OK. If possible, I want to talk with her."

Shannon's text made my phone vibrate, asking me if I was coming home soon. I replied I was on the way back and I'd rather be alone for the rest of today. All I wanted to do was sleep and not be haunted by nightmares anymore. That was my birthday wish.

We got off the highway and took a right onto Rock Road. St. Paul hospital was another quick right turn away, but Dad went right by it. Mom got out her cell phone and left a voicemail for Ms. Kim. I had avoided getting stuck with needles and pissing in cups for the time being, but I still needed answers.

"By the way," Dad began, "Uncle Charlie and Maverick are stopping by for a visit Monday evening. They're heading up to Chicago, so they decided to stay the night and hang out with us for a little bit."

Uncle Charlie was an aerospace genius or something, but he and Aunt Louise had divorced a little while ago, and I hadn't seen my cousin since before that happened. When she died in a horrible car accident last year, we drove down to Florida for the funeral, but Maverick wasn't there. He had been kidnapped or maybe ran away with some Satanic cult, but he came back home after a few weeks. They moved to Cape Girardeau, just two hours south of us, and I always wondered when I'd see Maverick again. After all my cousin had been through, I'm pretty sure he was probably the one person in the world more messed up than me.

"That's cool," I said. "I haven't seen Mav in a long time."

"Just be careful not to talk about his ordeal," Mom said.

Dad added, "Maybe you and your friends can take him out. Uncle Charlie said he doesn't have many friends in Cape."

"No problem," I replied. "Maybe he should see Ms. Kim too."

"Stop joking!" Mom reached back to slap me, but her arm was too short. "Your cousin has been through a lot. Poor Uncle Charlie. They are trying to piece their lives back together, so be nice."

I resisted rolling my eyes. "Of course, I'll be nice. We'll take Maverick out to a movie or something."

"Sounds good." Dad made a left onto our street. "Looks like we have company."

Shannon, Brandon, and Dylan sat on our front steps holding balloons and stuff, getting to their feet as we pulled up into our driveway.

"Isn't that sweet?" Mom's smile reached ear-to-ear. "You're lucky to have such great friends."

I sighed. "Yup. Very lucky."

Since I didn't get to eat all of my barbeque at Pop's, the cookie cake they had brought was extremely delicious. With my friends over, laughing and having a good time, Mom and Dad had forgotten all about my episode at the restaurant. For that, I was thankful. It was still nice out, so we went into my backyard and sat down at the large round patio table.

Shannon brought the remnants of the cookie cake outside while Brandon and Dylan hauled a cooler of soda into the yard. We had a good two hours of sunlight left, and my crankiness disappeared as I munched on another piece of the giant cookie.

"How was Pop's?" Brandon asked me. "They literally have the best ribs in the world."

I guess the look on my face was enough of an answer for them. "I passed out again."

"What?" Dylan popped open a can of orange soda. "Maybe you should have a CT scan. Might be a tumor."

"You sound just like my mom." I stopped to swallow the chocolatey goodness in my mouth. "No, it's not a too-mah!" I said in my very best

Schwarzenegger.

Shannon moved towards me from the other side of the table to stare into my eyes. "You look like shit, Jonah."

I laughed in her face. "Yeah. Happy Birthday to me."

"No, seriously." She sat back down and shook her head. "You've got dark circles around your eyes. You're like a zombie at school. Is it the nightmares?"

Without hesitation, I replied, "Yeah. Just about every night now."

Brandon's eyes widened. "You haven't seen…" He gestured upwards. "Have you?"

"No. No Mothman." I put my head down on my arms and let the cool breeze attempt to relax me. "I keep dreaming about Elijah. I see all of this destruction and death all over the place. The last one I had was really messed up. Elijah and the Mothman were in it, and a big red tornado."

Dylan looked like he was about to ask me something, but he put his soda can to his mouth instead.

"What were they doing in your dream?" Shannon asked.

"The Mothman just kept flying in circles above us, but Elijah kept saying this wasn't a dream. He said I was having visions. All the while, a tornado is just getting bigger and bigger. And a river of blood was nearby, and skeletons everywhere. In the middle of all this horror, Elijah told me the Cardinals beat the Reds 14-2."

The three of them stared at me as if I was crazy for a long time until Shannon finally said, "Sounds really messed up."

"And that's why I can't get any sleep."

Brandon reached over to grab a piece of the cookie cake. "It sounds terrible, except for the Cardinals whipping the Reds."

We all got a little laugh out of Brandon's comment, and we went back to talking about normal stuff. Brandon said there had been some local blogs talking about seeing UFOs in the area, but nothing about the Mothman yet. Shannon had some lady in a wheelchair fart while she was transporting her to the radiology department, and it had smelled like rotten bananas. Dylan looked exhausted, and he looked like he wanted to say something important but held back.

I told them my cousin, Maverick, was coming to town, and I wanted to take him to a movie or something later in the evening. Without giving any details, I told them Maverick had been through a lot, but as far as I remember, he was a cool guy. He was a year older than us, but he'd get along with everybody in the group. Unfortunately, none of them could make it since it was a school night.

After another hour or so, there wasn't much left of

the cookie cake, and the others said their goodbyes, except for Dylan. After Shannon and Brandon had left, he lingered for a bit, helping me clean up. I knew he had been holding something back all evening, and sure enough, he eventually summoned enough courage to tell me what had been bothering him.

"I'm having nightmares too."

I immediately felt guilty. Was whatever that was haunting me contagious or something? I sat back down, and it took Dylan a long time to give me some details about his dreams.

"Mine didn't have a tornado, but I did dream about the river of blood flowing all around. Skeletons and stuff too. The ground shook, buildings fell, and people died. It was bad."

I couldn't speak. In a selfish way, though, there was some comfort in knowing someone else knew exactly what I was going through. I wasn't alone anymore.

"In my nightmares, I see my grandfather. He's telling me to be prepared. I ask him for specifics, but he doesn't tell me anything more."

"Anything about the Cardinals beating the Reds?" I ask.

Dylan chuckled and took a final swig of his third orange soda of the night. "Nope. I've had the same recurring nightmare the last couple of nights. What do you think?"

"Maybe you should keep a notepad and pen next to your bed too," I answer. "Although it seems there's not a whole lot I forget about these dreams after I wake up."

We sat in silence for a little while, picking up the paper plates and soda cans before putting them into a trash bag. The sun was setting, and I actually did have a little homework. Dylan did too. He ran inside to thank Mom and Dad for letting them have this impromptu surprise party. I walked him to his car across the street, and I could tell he wanted to tell me more, but he had already said enough.

"Happy Birthday, Jonah," he said before he got into his truck.

"Thanks, man."

I watched him drive off, and I changed my birthday wish. I wished Dylan would be spared yet another nightmare tonight, so he could get some sleep. But I was no longer a child, and I didn't really believe in birthday wishes anymore.

CHAPTER 12

MS. KIM RODRIGUEZ had been my counselor since I was thirteen. Before her, I used to go to another lady, but she moved away. Mom had heard great things about Ms. Kim from one of her clients, and it was easy to see why. She had an easygoing, non-judgmental personality. Looking back at our sessions, she never really gave me advice. She just listened and asked questions. I probably did at least ninety percent of the talking. Ms. Kim simply let the silence hang in her comfortable office until I continued rambling.

It had been more than six months since I last met with her. Ms. Kim's office was only three miles away, tucked away in the corner of a small commercial building with ancient brick and tilted windows. After school, I drove myself to her office just as I had promised Mom and Dad.

When I arrived, I threw all my energy into pushing

aside my anxiety. In our past sessions, I simply spilled my guts. Ms. Kim never professed to solve all my problems, but just the very act of letting everything out was such a relief. This time, however, I had to pull back the reins and not bring up the Mothman and being visited by the Men in Black. Otherwise, she'd make the call to St. Paul's psyche ward, and I'd be institutionalized for sure.

The waiting room was stark white, and the chairs had to have been constructed in the 70s. Nothing was up on the walls, and various magazines going back to 2003 lay on small oak tables. I was the only one there. After checking in up front, I only had to wait a few minutes before being called in.

Ms. Kim's office was nearly as empty. I sat down on the microfiber couch and made myself comfortable. As always, I started talking about stuff happening in my everyday life. I described my anxiety about going away to college and making the right decision. Of course, I mentioned the pressure Mom was putting on me. Then, we discussed the stress most young adults at this point in their lives usually experience, and she gave me some great tips on some things I could do to help relieve my stress.

Our talk then turned to my nightmares and passing out at school and the restaurant. Ms. Kim seemed worried, and she asked me more medical questions, which freaked me out. I did describe my dreams, but I left out the Mothman stuff and how its glowing, red eyes seemed to sear themselves into my brain.

"Happy Birthday, by the way," Ms. Kim said with a smile. "So why do you think your eighteenth was so much harder than the previous birthdays."

The answer seemed obvious, but Ms. Kim never assumed anything. I replied, "I guess it's because I'm leaving my childhood behind. Elijah will always be a nine-year-old in my mind. I feel like I'm leaving him behind too."

"How do you feel like you're leaving him behind?"

I had to think about that one for a long time. "I often imagine what it'd be like if he were here. We'd be graduating high school together, maybe even go to the same college. We had such different personalities, so I assume we'd still be different from each other as adults too. Is that weird to be afraid to leave behind someone who's dead?"

Ms. Kim shrugged her slight shoulders. "Weird? No. Not weird at all. You are continuing to move forward in your life, and like you said, Elijah is still that nine-year-old boy you remember."

"Maybe that's the problem. I remember too much." I stopped to mull over my new revelation.

"You mean because of your hyperthymesia?" Ms. Kim asked.

It never took much effort to recall what had happened that day. "Yeah. It was a warm August day.

Mom had dressed us in identical navy-blue polo shirts and khaki shorts. A family with a golden retriever sat at a picnic table near the playground. Mom always hovered over us, but she told us to stay close to the restroom while she went in just for a quick moment. Elijah went crazy with his newfound freedom and ran off towards the walking trail. I, however, always followed the rules and didn't budge. Then a man with long, dirty blond hair followed him. The guy went with Elijah down the trail and disappeared into the trees. I ran towards them, and I was angry at my brother. We weren't supposed to talk to strangers."

My eyes were full of tears, which I wiped away with my hand. Ms. Kim's expression had changed. Normally, she was calm and stoic. She'd smile here and there, and that was about it. But now, just as she had on only a handful of occasions, she looked like she could truly feel my pain. In previous sessions, I had described what happened in bits and pieces. As crazy as this was, I had only shared half of the details my brain had recorded about that terrible day.

"If I wasn't able to remember all of the little details about Elijah being kidnapped, I don't think I'd be so messed up today."

Ms. Kim nodded. "We've talked about how you tend to relive that day over and over again, and how it seems to intensify as your birthday approaches. This year seems much harder for you, as you feel like you get to move on in your life and Elijah doesn't. Right?"

"Yeah." I had only needed to reach for the tissues on the table on two occasions, and I found myself grabbing a few. "I feel guilty, I guess. The guy could have easily taken me instead. I'll never forget the way Mom screamed when we couldn't find him. I know she feels guilty too, which is why she's overprotective of me now. She was always this way, but now it's ten times worse after everything that's happened."

Ms. Kim seemed concerned, and she talked about referring me to a psychiatrist. My condition had taken a medical turn for the worse, and she was concerned about my lack of sleep. She said something about the body reacting to anxiety and stress just as if I had an actual illness, and medication might be a way to help me.

I hated the idea of having to take meds, but I knew she'd be following up with Mom, so I tried my best to hide my disappointment.

Driving home was a blur. Ms. Kim's office was only ten minutes away, and I went into autopilot, which was scary. I didn't remember the drive home. I shook myself awake from my mental fog when I pulled up onto the driveway and noticed a strange SUV parked there.

Uncle Charlie and Maverick were here.

Maverick was more talkative than I remembered. Especially with all the tragedy he'd been through in the last year, I expected him to be this quiet, fragile guy. But he was far from shy. As we drove to the movie theater, he talked about his girlfriend, Lisa, who was going to Florida State, and how he planned to follow her for the spring semester. He described how Cape Girardeau was so different from living in Florida. He asked about me, what I'd been up to. The small talk was actually pretty great. Therapeutic even. But underneath all of that, I think we knew we were both broken people who had a lot of crap to deal with.

"I'm sorry about your mom," I said as I turned into the theater's parking lot.

Maverick was silent for a moment. "Thanks. My dad said you guys came to the funeral."

I was supposed to not bring up anything even remotely related to the crazy stuff Maverick had to deal with: his mom's death, him running away with a cult, or his dad losing his big job. Instead, I didn't say anything at all. I got the feeling he knew I was trying to choose my words carefully.

"Hey, Happy Birthday, man," Maverick finally said. "Eighteen now. A man!"

The parking lot was barren. Monday night was

probably the slowest night for the movies. I turned off the air conditioner and killed the engine. "Yup. I feel pretty manly."

We sat quietly long enough for most people to start feeling uncomfortable, but I didn't feel uneasy at all. I could tell Maverick didn't mind the silence either. Maybe we were both so preoccupied with trying not to trigger any kind of emotional breakdown between the two of us.

"My dad told me not to bring up Elijah," Maverick confessed. As if he could read my mind, he added, "And I'm pretty sure your parents told you not to bring up the whole cult thing or my mom dying."

I couldn't help but laugh awkwardly. "Yeah. That's about right."

Maverick took a deep breath. "I've been through hell, man. It has been a rough year. I know you haven't had it easy either. So, we kind of get each other, right?"

"For sure." I looked into my cousin's eyes, and I felt like I could tell him anything. "I've got some great friends, but they don't really understand."

"That's great. Having friends, I mean," Maverick said. "You're a lucky guy. Even if they can't relate, you should still talk to them and stuff."

"I do." The action flick we were going to catch was going to start in three minutes, but I got the feeling we were going to miss it. "How about you? Make any new friends down in Cape?"

Maverick shook his head. "I lost a lot of my friends. Lisa gets me, though." He threw me a sly smile. "If you're curious about anything, you can ask. It's cool."

I stopped to make sure I said the right words, but I just came right out and asked him, "Why did you run away with a cult?"

For one fleeting moment, Maverick looked as if he was about to cry, but he busted out laughing in my face instead. I didn't know what the hell had just happened, so I laughed along with him. He wiped his eyes and caught his breath when he was done.

"Promise not to tell your parents?" he asked me.

"Of course."

"I didn't join a damn cult," Maverick said with a chuckle, then his face hardened. "Some terrible things happened all at once. My mom died, my best friend was killed, and Lisa's best friend died too. All within a matter of days of each other."

I felt like I had been punched in the stomach. "Holy shit."

Maverick was about to continue his story, but something outside caught his attention. His gaze was locked on something out in the distance. I tried to see what he was looking at, but there was a glare on my part of the windshield from the parking lot lights.

"What is it?" I asked.

Without answering me, Maverick opened the

passenger door and got out of the car. I thought maybe a carjacker was about to target us, so I jumped out ready for a fight. Instead, an old car's headlights lit us up from the other side of the parking lot. It crept slowly towards us until it stopped just a few feet from the front of my car. It was a black Mercedes.

Maverick crossed his arms and whispered, "Damn you."

Both doors opened, and the two Men in Black stepped out. They were still dressed in dark navy-blue suits, and the guy with the slicked back hair left the driver's side to stand toe-to-toe with Maverick. The other spook with the old fedora stayed back next to the car with both of his hands hidden behind the door.

"What do you idiots want?" Maverick asked them.

I didn't understand why Maverick was so cocky to these guys. Most people, including myself, would've been having a meltdown right about then. It was dark out, yet they were still wearing their black sunglasses. The strangest part was the sound of static filling my head again. Maverick didn't seem to be bothered by it, however.

"Going to catch a movie?" black-haired man asked with a grin.

"What do most people do when they go to a movie theater?" Maverick still wasn't fazed. "Why don't you leave us alone? We're not doing anything to anybody."

I wondered if the guy with the gray fedora had a

gun or something behind the door. "They're with UFOIL," I told my cousin.

Maverick let out a fake laugh that reminded me of Jim Carrey in Ace Ventura. "UFOIL?"

The black-haired man put his hands on his hips, "UFO Investigators League."

Maverick's bravery was contagious, so I blurted out, "Bogus, man. UFOIL shut down years ago."

Fedora guy asked us, "Have you seen anything unusual lately?"

Maverick looked as if he might actually take a swing at the black-haired guy. "You mean, other than you two gangsters driving around at night wearing shades? No, but then again, I just got into town, which I'm sure you already knew."

Did Maverick know something I didn't know?

The black-haired man turned to me. "How about you, Jonah? Have you seen anything unusual lately? Maybe something in the sky?"

I didn't like how he knew my name. "Even if I did, I'm not telling you guys a damn thing."

Both spooks exchanged exasperated looks before getting back into their car. The black-haired man stuck his head out of the window and said, "Enjoy the movie, Maverick."

The Mercedes slid backwards before turning away and exiting the parking lot.

"I hate those guys," Maverick said while watching

them turn onto Rock Road.

I had been holding my breath, so I let myself exhale. "Me and my friends had a run in with them just a couple of days ago at Wells Park."

"Really?" Maverick's eyes narrowed. "What did they want?"

"They asked us if we'd seen UFOs and stuff." I wondered how much to tell Maverick, but it was easy telling him everything. "They are creepy as hell."

"So, have you?" he asked me.

"Have I what?"

"Have you seen UFOs and stuff?"

My hesitation probably answered his question, but I replied, "Yeah. Me and my friends have been seeing some crazy stuff up in the sky lately, but it's obvious those two Men in Black aren't with UFOIL." I looked him straight in the eyes. "You know them, don't you? They seemed to know you, that's for sure.

After a short sigh, Maverick replied, "They're with a top-secret government agency known as Level 6. If they're hot on your tail, you are screwed, Cuz."

CHAPTER 13

THE ACTION MOVIE we were supposed to watch was at least halfway over by the time I finished telling Maverick everything. I totally spilled my guts about the very first Mothman sighting the others and I had, my nightmares and visions, the passing out episodes, and meeting the Mothman itself face-to-face. Amazingly, Maverick never laughed or rolled his eyes. He listened just as intently as Ms. Kim always did, and he was never once judgmental. When I finished my story with how we met the Men in Black at Wells Park, Maverick finally spoke.

"They're wearing blue suits, though."

I couldn't argue there. "It still works, but Men in Black sounds better than the Men in Blue."

Maverick took a moment to let all of my information soak in, and I actually felt better than I had in a long time. Mom was right. Holding all of this stuff in was just tearing me up inside. Finally being able to tell someone else outside my circle of friends was such a relief.

"Like I said, they are agents of a government organization called Level 6," Maverick said.

I asked him, "How do you know them?"

Maverick seemed to struggle with figuring how much to tell me. He scrunched his mouth in contemplation before replying, "My dad used to work for them, indirectly. He worked alongside Level 6."

"Uncle Charlie is a Man in Black?"

My uncle was just about as boring and quiet as my dad. It was amazing how two brothers could be so alike. They were identical twins, too. Unlike me and Elijah, they were very similar. Both were soft-spoken and overly logical. Dad decided to go become a financial guy, but Uncle Charlie went the aerospace engineering route. I had a feeling either one could have gone to do each other's job with the right schooling.

"No, Jonah." Maverick leaned in close, putting his right arm on the steering wheel. "The less you know, the better. But what I'm about to tell you, you have to take to the grave. Got it?"

I nodded. My hands got sweaty just waiting for whatever secrets Maverick had been keeping. "I told you my crazy-ass story already. Now it's your turn."

"My dad worked on a top-secret military project. You know how he designed airplanes and stuff, so I'll just let you use your imagination as to what kinds of out-of-this-world aircraft he was designing."

My brain exploded with possibilities. I immediately thought of Area 51 and high tech flying machines utilizing technologies reverse-engineered from aliens. Being a science fiction aficionado, my imagination didn't have to stretch very far.

"Level 6 is the muscle for many of the government's Dark Projects. Their job is to make sure the people over here don't know what the hell the people over there are doing. Not even the president of the United States knows what's going on. They call it compartmentalization. Ignorance is bliss. Underneath these secret projects are even darker, more sinister projects going on."

"Like what?" I asked.

Maverick shook his head. "Again, the less you know, the better. Just know these dark projects are terrible. They even experiment on children. My dad had no idea what was happening under his nose, and Level 6 kept it that way. These guys are bad news. They are responsible for my mom's death and three of my friends' deaths too. I got mixed up in all that shit, and it's why we left Florida and moved to Missouri."

I had a million questions, but I knew Maverick wouldn't answer them.

"I've seen them around town down in Cape Girardeau, and they make sure I can see them tailing me. Watching me."

A new realization made my heart jump. "If they killed Aunt Louise and your friends and got away with it, they can pretty much do whatever they want."

"They're very good at cleaning up after themselves," Maverick said. "The whole cult thing is a bunch of bull crap, but it helped explain away the disappearance of my friends. Level 6 is thorough, and they will do whatever it takes to keep you quiet."

A second revelation just about pushed me into panic mode. "You think the Mothman is one of Level 6's experiments? Maybe it got loose or something?"

Maverick continued, "Maybe. I wouldn't doubt it. But understand this: there's a reason why they keep asking you about what you've seen. You can play dumb for only so long. Level 6 is onto you and your friends."

I went back to our first encounter with Level 6 at Wells Park, and maybe Maverick could help me solve one of the mysteries surrounding those spooks. "When those two agents first interrogated us at the park, all of us could hear a loud static sound in our heads. I felt it again tonight when they showed up here. What's up with that?"

Maverick said, "Some of the Dark Projects have to do with psionic warfare. Weaponizing extra sensory perception. Did you also feel like you were being pushed against your will?"

"Hell yeah."

"The agents following you aren't just a couple of guys hired to spy on people and assassinate enemies. I suspect they were actually bred by Level 6, their genetics altered to give them mind control abilities."

All of this was just crazy. "They were bred?"

"Most of these Dark Projects throw morality right out the window," Maverick replied. "I don't want to put you in any more danger by telling you everything that happened with me. I often wonder why Level 6 doesn't just kill me and Dad, but I think it's because I've made some pretty badass friends who could, if pissed off enough, bring them down."

Maverick had a big story to tell. Even though he couldn't give me details, I was grateful he filled in a few blanks for me. At least I had a better idea of what we were up against. "What should I do?"

"The world is nothing like I thought it was." Maverick looked out the passenger window. "I don't know how everything you're dealing with is connected to my story, but all I know is that it is. Your visions of the end of the world and Elijah talking to you, the Mothman, Level 6 trying to get information out of you, and your fainting episodes—they're all connected. Welcome to my world, Cuz." He turned to look me in the eyes. "Just keep your mind open. You're getting slapped around from all sides right now, I totally get it."

Maverick was right. I was running scared. "Keep

my mind open to the possibilities."

"My dad said you've got straight A's. You're a smart dude. You've got a sharp mind, but maybe you also need to open your heart more too. With your wits and an open heart, you'll figure it all out."

"Open my heart?"

"We all have that little voice inside our heads. It's our intuition. Our gut. Use it, Jonah. When you have your next vision, don't just try to decipher Elijah's cryptic messages. Allow yourself to feel, and your instincts will help you take it all in. You'll see and feel things you might have missed before."

I glanced at the digital clock in the car, and it was already almost ten. "I've got school tomorrow." I turned the ignition and turned on the headlights. "I wish you guys were staying longer."

"Me too, Cuz." Maverick pulled his seatbelt across his chest. "Dad doesn't allow me to have a phone, but I have a disposable one anyway. It's how I still talk to Lisa. We've got a system where we throw the phones away after a few weeks. It's for her own protection."

Normally, I would have thought such a practice was paranoia, but now I totally understood why. "Makes sense."

Maverick said, "Give me your cell later, and I'll put in my number. Just don't use my real name in your contacts list, OK?"

"Yeah. Good idea." I put the car in drive and rolled

towards the parking lot exit. "What's funny is how your name is already a codename, so I'll have to give you an inconspicuous one. Like Bob or Jim."

"If you need anything, just let me know, but I can't guarantee I'll answer your call right away. I have to make sure Dad isn't around. He'd kill me if he found out I had a phone."

Just to make sure, I surveyed the area for the black Mercedes. "Thanks, man. I appreciate it."

"You're not alone, Jonah." Maverick turned his head in all directions as if he was looking for the Level 6 agents too. "Make sure your buddies know about Level 6 and stuff. Whatever they do, they cannot admit to seeing or knowing anything."

Were they in danger too? Now guilt started to settle in. What if I had dragged them into this mess? I could never forgive myself if something were to happen to Shannon, Brandon, or Dylan because of me.

Maverick tapped my shoulder. "Don't be so hard on yourself, Cuz. There's no room for guilt right now. Just keep an open mind and heart, and make sure you and your friends stick together."

I stopped the car, even though the light was green. "Can you read minds or something?"

A wide smile spread on Maverick's face. "That's a story for another day."

Uncle Charlie and Maverick each took a couch in our living room, and I lay in my own bed, unable to stop my brain from going a thousand miles an hour. For once, I hoped to actually have another dream. This time, I would take Maverick's advice and try to keep an open mind and heart. I would pay closer attention to how I felt during these visions. Maybe that was the key to solving all of these mysteries.

After about an hour of trying to get my body to relax, my phone's vibrating pulled me from the very edge of sleep. The screen said, "UNKNOWN," and I never answered those calls. My gut said to answer it anyway, so I did.

"Hello?" All I could hear was static at first. But I thought maybe I heard someone breathing. "Hello?"

The voice coming out of my phone sounded faraway, as if it was straining to cut through all the static. "Elijah."

I nearly dropped the phone. "Hello? Who is this?"

"It's Jonah."

The voice had so much interference around it, I couldn't figure out who was playing this stupid prank on me. "I'm Jonah, you idiot. Who the hell is this?"

The static died down long enough for the voice to come through crystal clear. "It's me."

"Elijah?" I sat up straight in bed. It took all of my strength to just listen and stop trying to analyze everything. Open mind. Open heart. "I recognize your voice." Such a stupid thing to say since Elijah and I had identical voices. This wasn't nine-year-old Elijah who had called me. This was the Elijah who was eighteen now.

His voice sliced through the interference again. "The poison."

I took a deep breath, pushing back the urge to ask all kinds of questions. So, I simply repeated, "The poison."

"In the earth."

"The poison in the earth," I whispered. "OK."

"He will need you."

Elijah had said the same thing before in one of my previous dreams, and I had to force my mouth shut to not ask him who would need me.

"When the poison in the earth is unleashed, he will need you."

My brother's voice started to fade. I panicked. "Who? Who will need me? What does the Mothman have to do with all of this? What's going on, Elijah? Just tell me. Please!"

The only reply I got was an earful of static, and the line went dead.

CHAPTER 14

UNCLE CHARLIE AND Maverick had left the house early the next morning, barely grabbing a little breakfast before hitting the road to get to Chicago before lunchtime. Maverick had given me his secret cell phone number under the alias "Luke Skywalker" and he asked Uncle Charlie if they could possibly stop by for a longer visit on their way back home from Chicago. If it worked out, they'd stay next weekend.

When they left, I was eager to talk to the others and let them know everything Maverick had told me about Level 6. I had a nightmare-less night for the first time in days, although the late-night phone call more than made up for it. I felt more like myself since I had gotten a good eight hours of sleep. My plan was to text the others to meet at the school's parking lot at least half an hour before the first warning bell, but I could tell something was bothering Dad at the table.

I asked him, "What's up? Did you have a good visit with your bro?"

Dad normally never used his cell phone at the table, but he frowned when he scrolled down to read something. "Um, yes. Yes, we did. He and Maverick are settling nicely down in Cape, and he's visiting with an old colleague up in Chi-Town. How was the movie?"

Mom walked into the kitchen with her laptop. "Was it any good?"

"Not really, but it was really cool hanging out with Maverick. We've got a lot in common."

"I'm glad you two got along so well," Dad said. "No wonder he wanted to come back and visit after their trip. Life has been rough for your cousin, and Uncle Charlie said he never really made good friends down in Cape. Maybe things will get a little easier for him when he starts college."

Dad sighed before putting his phone away.

"What's wrong, William?" Mom asked.

"There's a big demonstration near the office, which means all kinds of traffic on our street. It took me a good two hours to get to work the last time there was such a ruckus at the landfill." Dad took a sip of his coffee. "I'm in complete agreement with the protestors, but it's a pain dealing with all the commotion."

Mom clicked her tongue and put her laptop in her

bag. "The smell has been horrid this past summer. I was showing a house downwind from the stench, and my buyers didn't want anything to do with the entire subdivision. It's such a shame. It's killing home values."

I was probably just about as informed as any regular resident of Bridgetowne, and in the last few years, there was growing discussion about it at school. Shannon, being a member of the Ecology Club, was much more informed on the issue than the rest of us. Other than the horrible smell, I hadn't put a lot of thought about the landfill until I had my Mothman encounter near Dad's office.

Mom said, "You need to move."

"We've looked into it, but it would be an expensive move. It's hard to find affordable warehousing space around here. We might have to go across the river." Dad stood up and felt his pockets for his wallet and car keys. "Maybe if it causes enough disturbance in our operations, it'll give us enough incentive to move."

"I don't know how you tolerate the smell," Mom said. "Your employees keep the warehouse doors open, which allows the odor to blow in." She turned to me with a scowl. "I'm sure you smell it too at school."

"Sometimes," I replied. "If it's really hot and the wind is blowing just right. Freshman year, we smelled it just about every time we went out for gym class."

Mom stood up and went to the kitchen to dump the

rest of her coffee down the drain. "It's that poison in the earth. I hope the EPA stops giving us the runaround and admits the issue needs to be remedied."

I nearly choked on my pop tart. Poison in the earth. "I got to go. I forgot I had to talk to Mr. Reynolds before school." I grabbed my backpack and car keys from the counter. Before heading out, I told Dad: "Be careful going into work. Those protesters can get crazy."

He gave me the thumbs up. "Will do."

I fumbled with my phone as I hurried out the door and got into my car. Shannon could help me catch up on the landfill issue, so I needed to reach out to her first.

Poison in the earth.

I was finally on the verge of putting one of the pieces of this mystery together.

"Maverick." Brandon savored my cousin's name as if he had taken a bite out of a pepperoni pizza. "That is literally the coolest name ever."

I slapped his shoulder. "Focus, man."

Dylan looked haggard. His eye lids were swollen, and he seemed as if he might collapse had he not been leaning up against my car for support. "Sounds like your cousin had a major run-in with these Level 6 guys before."

"Big time," I said. "He kept all the details out, but from what he told me, they will go to great lengths to keep the truth from getting out there."

Shannon fiddled with her ponytail. "The part that creeps me out the most is how these agents can invade our minds and try to get us to talk. It's disturbing."

"Maverick said to make sure to play dumb. You have to concentrate on resisting their mind-bending." The parking lot was starting to fill up, and we had maybe a couple minutes until the first bell. "I'm really sorry if I dragged you all into this."

"It's not your fault," Dylan said. "We were all together when we first saw it flying around the mall. From the very beginning, we were all involved."

Brandon continued reading something on his phone. "Yeah, but the rest of us haven't had a private visit from the Mothman." He looked up with wide eyes. "Yet, anyway."

Shannon play-punched my shoulder. "You're special, Jonah."

"There's one more thing," I said in a low voice. "Elijah called me last night."

All three of them looked at me as if I had a big-ass horn coming out of my forehead.

"It was all staticky at first, but I heard my brother's voice clear as day." Even though it was a warm morning, a chill danced on the back of my neck. "He told me when the poison in the earth is unleashed, he will need me."

"Who will need you?" Shannon asked.

"I have no idea."

Dylan's face already looked discolored, but his complexion started taking on a greenish hue. "Poison in the earth?"

I said, "This morning, my parents were talking about the demonstration at the landfill today. Those things block traffic, and my dad's office is right there. And my mom talked about how the stench was affecting home values in the area."

Shannon snapped her fingers. "That makes perfect sense. With the underground fire inching towards all the radioactive crap, we're getting closer and closer to unleashing the poison. Me and a couple other Ecology Club members are going to join the demonstration after school today; maybe you guys should come too."

"You think the Mothman is going to show up?" Brandon asked.

"I doubt it," I replied. "But all of this is definitely connected to the landfill. Just need to figure out how. According to Elijah, when the shit hits the fan, someone is going to need my help. It's like one big puzzle, and I'm not sure I have all the pieces."

Before anyone could even begin to speculate, the first warning bell echoed from the building. Brandon and Shannon's first class was clear on the other side of campus, so they hurried into school. Dylan lingered behind, and the color still hadn't returned to his face.

"You look like shit, man," I told him.

Dylan looked too tired to laugh. "Something happened to me last night."

"Another vision?"

He shook his head and pulled out his phone. "My dead grandpa called my phone too."

In three years of high school, I had only been tardy to first hour three times. That day would be number four. I felt my face turn hot, and it took me a second or two to gather my thoughts.

"Are you for real?" was all I could muster.

"He died five years ago. We were pretty close."

Dylan's eyes fluttered, and I felt terrible for him. I asked him, "What did he say?"

"Amazingly, something similar to what Elijah told you. He said the word poison and earth a bunch of times. The static coming from the phone was loud, but those two words were pretty distinct. My grandpa also said: 'She will need you.' It's messed up, I know."

Had Dylan misinterpreted his grandfather's message since he heard *she* instead of *he*? Or was he getting an ominous warning that was related, yet separate from mine?

"What do you think, Jonah?"

I didn't want to freak Dylan out any more than he was, but I had to think out loud. "I've been getting warnings from Elijah, and now you are from your dead grandfather. It's obvious, isn't it? They know something bad is going to happen. Something terrible. Maybe the underground fire is going to hit the radioactive waste at the landfill, like Shannon said, sending poison into the air or something."

Dylan's weary eyes flashed understandingly. "Since the Mothman started appearing all around Point Pleasant just before the Silver Bridge collapsed, it makes sense it's come to St. Louis to warn us of a terrible disaster too. It has to be the landfill."

The tardy bell rang, but we were just one of at least a dozen stragglers in the parking lot.

"Thanks for not calling me crazy," Dylan said with a smirk.

I led us towards our long walk to the school's lobby doors. "Are you kidding? If anyone else were to find out the stuff I've seen, I'd be eating lunch today in a padded cell."

"Should we hurry?" Dylan had never been late to class, ever.

"We're already late," I replied.

Maverick said it was important for me to listen to my intuition. A strong, compelling feeling that we shouldn't go into the building came over me. The hairs on my arms stood up the closer we got to the front doors.

Dylan stopped in his tracks. "What's wrong?"

"I'm not sure," I answered in a whisper. "I just don't think we should go inside right now."

"Are you playing with me? I'm not in a good place right now for this kind of crap." Dylan surged ahead of me and took three strides towards the building. "Let's go!"

I couldn't move.

My rational mind started to take over, and I took a hesitant step towards Dylan. And the moment I did, a piercing alarm penetrated the brick building and rattled our brains. We stood motionless, just staring at each other.

"What the hell?" Dylan retreated back to my side. "What's going on?"

All of the lobby doors swung open, and a stampede of students and teachers rushed outside. Dylan and I had to move out of the way to avoid being trampled. Every teacher led their students out of the building, through the outdoor patio, and out into the grass near the parking lot.

Someone had pulled the fire alarm.

CHAPTER 15

WE HAD TO park a good three miles away from my dad's building because of all the traffic coming from the Rock Road. Although the protesting began early in the morning, there was plenty of action going on by the time we had arrived. The police were busy rounding up about a dozen hardcore protesters who had chained themselves to a bunch of barrels and blocked the entrance to the landfill.

This part of town was a maze of industrial streets crisscrossing each other right next to the smelly dump. Since Dad's building was directly across the street, if the protests didn't die down by five o'clock, he'd probably be late coming home too.

News vans lined the streets, as did all the police cars. Shannon was busy on her phone texting somebody important. The rest of us were mesmerized by all the angry banners and signs the protesters carried. We were lucky to find an empty picnic bench in the back of one of the buildings, allowing us to get a great view of everything going on.

"I told Mrs. Kelly where we were," Shannon said as she put her phone away. "She's on her way."

"Mrs. Kelly?" Brandon asked. "Psychology teacher?"

Shannon nodded. "And our Ecology Club sponsor. She's been here all day."

I had never taken psychology, so I didn't have Mrs. Kelly. But she was a popular teacher. She sponsored Ecology Club and Key Club, and even though she wasn't much older than my parents, she was rumored to be retiring soon. Mrs. Kelly must've started teaching right out of college. After a few minutes, she emerged from the crowd gathered near the landfill's entrance. She was a petite lady, and it looked like she might get knocked over by the chanting people jumping up and down all around her.

"Thanks for taking a break from the protest," Shannon said as she made room on the picnic bench for Mrs. Kelly. "My friends are very concerned about the landfill, and they want to learn more about it. I could have given them a quick overview, but I thought they might have some questions you could answer."

Mrs. Kelly nodded and sat down. "No problem. My feet are killing me anyway."

"We all live nearby, and we are familiar with the

smell coming out of here during hot summer days," I said. "In history class, Mr. Klaas talked about the Manhattan Project and how all the radioactive waste from uranium enrichment ended up in the landfill. Other than that, we don't know much else."

"Congratulations," Mrs. Kelly began. "You are more educated than most. Let me start with the basics. All that waste includes some of the deadliest radiotoxic waste products in the world. Mr. Klaas taught you well. All this waste being stored here is the result of illegal dumping by the Matzenbach Corporation starting in the 1940s."

Dylan asked her, "How can a pharmaceutical company be involved with uranium and stuff? My uncle used to work there, but he was a chemist working on pain meds."

"Matzenbach got its start from developing pharmaceuticals for radiological purposes," Mrs. Kelly answered. "It was through developing these products used in radiology that led to them developing a process to enrich uranium. They were the first to do it."

Brandon had been reading something on his phone, but he looked up to ask Mrs. Kelly, "What's going on with the underground fire?"

Mrs. Kelly replied, "Back in 2010, they discovered there was an exothermic reaction underground. To put it simply, it was a release of heat due to a chemical reaction. The fire has been spreading ever since."

"I don't get it," I said. "Why can't they just put out the fire?"

"It's not so easy," Mrs. Kelly answered. "It's not a normal fire with flames and such. It's a high-temperature, smoldering fire one-hundred and fifty feet below the surface where there's very little oxygen. It's going to have to burn itself out. The local fire department found heat signatures in the ground much closer to the deadly stuff than what was first reported. If the fire were to reach the waste, you're talking about a mass evacuation of the St. Louis area and points east."

"The long-term danger is obvious," Brandon said as he finally put away his phone. "That stuff can stay radioactive for a thousand years. But what could happen, say, tomorrow? What are the real dangers we might be looking at?"

Mrs. Kelly stopped to think about Brandon's question before giving her answer. "The radioactive waste shouldn't even be here in the first place. It's in a densely populated area, for one. Also, this whole area is in a floodplain just a little over a mile away from the Missouri River with no real barrier to stop any seeping of radioactivity into the water."

The four of us exchanged worried looks. We'd had a few floods in the greater St. Louis area the last several years. A big enough flood could easily sweep all the radioactive crap from the landfill into the Missouri River, destroying our main water source.

"How about a tornado?" I asked.

"The one that hit us back in 2011 was a close call. We dodged a bullet." Mrs. Kelly's phone vibrated, but she kept it in her pocket. "Had it hit the radioactive waste, it would have become a terrifying disaster on top of an already tragic situation. Imagine radon particles flying all over the place. Deadly fallout everywhere."

Brandon looked like he might piss his pants. "We've had a few tremors lately, but how would a big earthquake affect the landfill?"

"We've got the New Madrid fault near us, and it's overdue. If we were to have a major earthquake, say a 7.0, the landfill could completely collapse. The earthquake would lead to a liquefaction of soil and toxic materials. Basically, the ground becomes like quicksand. There's no kind of engineered liner separating the toxic waste from groundwater. We're looking at massive contamination of our drinking water."

Mrs. Kelly's phone vibrated again, and after checking it, she stood up to get a better look at the protesters a mere fifty yards away. "That's my husband, and he's in the middle of all the commotion. I'd better get back to business."

After we thanked her, Mrs. Kelly darted towards

the landfill and disappeared into the crowd.

"Scary stuff," Brandon said. "It's hard to believe this thing is only five miles from my house."

Shannon nudged my arm. "What do you think? You believe Elijah was warning you about the landfill?"

I didn't have to think about my answer. "Yeah. Without a doubt."

Dylan slammed his hand down on the picnic table to get our attention. "Look over there!"

We turned to where he was pointing, and just down the road from us was the black Mercedes. It came to a halt not too far from where my car was parked. It stayed there for a long while until both doors opened. Sure enough, the black-haired agent and the fedora-wearing spook stepped out.

"What should we do?" Brandon looked ready to bolt at any moment.

The two agents stood next to their car and leaned against it, not moving as if they were statues. Since they still had their sunglasses on, I couldn't tell exactly where they were looking. They didn't make a move towards us, so it would have looked extra suspicious had we just gotten up and left.

"We can't just run off," I reply. "That'll look really bad. Let's just stay put and see how long they'll watch us."

Brandon fiddled with his phone. "Which reminds

me, on the UFO Network, others in town have reported having a run in with Level 6 too."

Dylan asked, "What did they say?"

One of them said they were at Wells Park, and the Level 6 agents interrogated the poster. He said they were asking if he'd seen anything in the sky. He told them he'd seen a UFO the night before, so he described the triangular object to Level 6. They left him alone after that."

"So now we're dealing with UFOs?" Shannon threw her hands up the air. "As if the Mothman wasn't enough."

"There have literally been seven reports of UFOs coming from the St. Louis area just in the last twenty-four hours," Brandon reported. "Something messed up is going on."

Dylan wiped away the cold sweat from his forehead. "I think I'm going to lose my mind."

I turned back to the agents, but they had disappeared. Their black car was still there. "I lost sight of them. Anybody see where they went?"

The others swiveled their heads in all directions, but no one could find them.

"I don't like this," Shannon said as she stood up. "I don't see them anywhere."

I swallowed the lump in my throat. "We can't just leave now. We have to walk right past their Mercedes to get to my car."

"What should we do now?" Shannon whined.

Dad's office was just on the other side of the street. "Let's go to my dad's office for just a little bit. We can wait in there until we know for sure Level 6 is gone."

Without saying a word, the others nodded and followed me to the street. After taking one last survey of the area, we hurried towards my dad's huge warehouse. Behind every dumpster and every building, I kept expecting the agents to jump out and shoot us with their silenced pistols. The front door to the building was already open, and I led them into the lobby. I kicked the doorstopper away and let the glass door close behind us.

No Level 6 and no gunshots. We were safe for the time being.

CHAPTER 16

THE PROTESTING EVENTUALLY died down enough for Dad to leave the office on time, but we decided to stick around for a little bit after the crowds and media left. The black Mercedes was also gone. We hurried across the street to the landfill, with nothing but a tall fence separating us from radioactive waste. I half-expected the Level 6 agents to suddenly appear and throw us into their car, but they had actually left. Only a few stragglers remained, but even they decided to stop protesting as the sun began to dip below the horizon.

All four of us kept our cell phones out and our gazes up towards the sky, just in case the Mothman was to make an appearance.

Brandon reported, "Just a minute ago, on our neighborhood Facebook page, two people have reported seeing UFOs near the mall."

"Why just UFOs?" Dylan asked. "But no

Mothman?"

I threw a rock at the caution sign, hitting it square in the center of the radioactive warning trefoil symbol. "Just a month ago, we would have given anything to see a UFO."

Dylan took some video footage of the huge covered mound. "I've got something to tell you guys." He slipped his phone into his side pocket, and he kept nervously scratching the back of his neck. "Jonah isn't the only one having crazy-ass dreams and stuff. I started having them too, just a couple of days ago."

Brandon pointed at me. "Are they just like his?"

"Pretty much." Dylan glanced at the landfill before continuing. "Very similar. Dead bodies everywhere. A river of blood. Massive storms toppling buildings. But that's not the worst of it."

Shannon moved to be at Dylan's side and patted his back. "You've looked really rough the last four mornings. I had just that one nightmare right after we first saw the Mothman, but you two are going through something next-level. What happened, Dylan?"

Dylan's head hung low. "I also got a really messed up phone call."

"From who?" Brandon asked him.

"My grandfather," Dylan replied. "He's been gone a couple years now. He gave me a message nearly identical to Jonah's. He talked about the poison in the earth, and that she would need me when the time came."

Shannon looked as if she was about to get sick. "This is a whole new level of weird."

"Yeah, but I feel we're close to figuring this all out," I said. "People all over town are reporting UFO sightings now. All my dreams and passing out, the landfill threat, and now the cryptic messages from those who have passed...it's all connected. Just like Point Pleasant, it's like there's some kind of psychic awakening happening, and there's a purpose to all of this."

"It's to help get us prepared," Dylan added. "Psychic awakening is right." He turned to me with a smile. "Tell them what happened this morning before school."

Brandon and Shannon gawked at me as if they expected me to tell them I could fly or something.

"It's not that big of deal," I said.

Shannon rushed over and gave me a sharp jab to my stomach. "Tell us!"

"After you and Brandon went into the school building, Dylan and I were talking about the phone call he had gotten from his dead grandfather. Then, the tardy bell rang, and we made our way to the school, but I had this strong feeling we shouldn't bother."

"That's asking for trouble," Brandon remarked. "Dylan's never late."

"Right. I just knew we shouldn't go through those

lobby doors."

Shannon asked me, "What did you do?"

"I just stood there, dumbfounded," I answered. "And a second later, the fire alarm went off."

"Everybody evacuated," Dylan continued. "It was a very Nostradamus-like moment."

Brandon came up to my face as if he was examining my eyes. "Did you know the fire alarm was going to go off?"

I pushed him away from me. "No, Brandon. I didn't know what specifically was going to happen. I just knew it was a waste of time to go in, since we were just going to have to go right back out anyway. I wasn't even counted tardy this morning."

Dylan threw a rock at the same caution sign, but he didn't even come close to hitting it. "Same here."

"OK, so now Jonah's a fortune teller," Shannon said with a smirk. "I'd feel better if we'd catch some real evidence of the Mothman, though."

"I'm with you there," I said. "I think we should still try to get it on video, so we can post it up. Maybe people are calling the Mothman a UFO. If others are seeing it and they too are having nightmares and visions, then either the entire city is having a mental breakdown or we're all being made to get prepared for something really bad that's going to happen."

"Should we be stocking up on water and food and stuff?" Shannon asked the group.

Dylan replied, "With the tornados we've had in recent history and the threat of a huge earthquake looming over the region for the last few years, it never hurts to be ready anyway."

I checked my phone, and it was almost seven o'clock. "I got to get home. I've actually got a ton of homework. Can you guys meet at my house after dinner tomorrow? Let's head back here and stake it out to try and catch the Mothman on video. In the meantime, we all should be keeping a notebook and a pen by our beds to write down our dreams. If you wait until you actually get out of bed, you'll forget. Bigger picture, we all need to be stocking up on water, food, maybe a battery-operated radio and flashlights. All that emergency stuff. Just tell your parents it's part of a school project if they should ask."

Brandon tapped my shoulder and pointed towards the street. "Our buddies are back."

The black Mercedes came to a halt inside Dad's company's parking lot. Neither agent got out, but they stared at us through their windshield from across the street. I led the others towards my car. I refused to give the agents a reason to chase us, so we walked as if we were on an innocent evening stroll. When we were a mere ten yards or so from my Camry, the corner of the building blocked us from Level 6's sight, so we sprinted to my car.

As I drove back towards school, the others kept

staring out the rear windshield. I held my breath the entire drive, but thankfully, Level 6 didn't tail us. They were playing mind games with us, just like Maverick said they would. Eventually, they would make their move.

And I would be ready for them.

CHAPTER 17

"I FORGOT TO tell you," Mom said as she worked at her laptop while on the couch. "We have an appointment to see a new doctor on Friday."

After dinner, Dad usually retreated to his home office for an hour before relaxing in front of the TV, but tonight, he seemed extra weary. Instead, he lay on the other couch across from Mom with his head on a throw pillow. He craned his neck to see my reaction.

"That's cool," I said as I grabbed my backpack.

"Ms. Kim and I talked for a while, and we agree you need a little help with lowering your anxiety," Mom said. "Maybe you'll be able to get more sleep and the fainting spells will go away."

I decided to throw them a bone. "Sounds good. I think you're right."

Mom's left eyebrow raised. "I'm glad you're not going to fight us on this."

"We'll just try the doctor's suggestions," Dad chimed in. "There's often a little trial and error with these kinds of things. It's not forever, Jonah. Just until you consistently feel better."

"Speaking of feeling better, what's up with you, Dad?"

"All the protesting was such a distraction," he replied. "The warehouse employees weren't very productive today. Everything just seemed to take longer."

Mom wagged a tiny finger at me. "I don't like you hanging out at those protests. They might turn violent."

"It was for school, Mom." It was a half-truth, since Mrs. Kelly was a teacher, after all. "I learned a lot about the dangers buried underground just a few feet from Dad's office. It's scary stuff. The EPA keeps saying everything is just fine, but they keep finding contaminated soil outside their so-called safe zone."

"It's good to learn about real life issues," Dad said to Mom. "It was all under control. The kids actually came to the office and hung out for a little bit until the crowd died down."

Dad closed his eyes and rubbed his forehead.

"Dad, are you having trouble sleeping?" I asked him.

Mom never gave him a chance to answer. "Yes, he is. I'm living in a house full of insomniacs."

"We might be acquiring one of our competitors in Minneapolis," Dad replied. "I've been stressed out over the financials."

I was going to ask if he'd been having strange dreams, but I decided not to. As I carried my backpack to my room, A sinking feeling something terrible was going to happen tonight sucked the air out my lungs. I had planned on listening to some relaxing music in bed to help me sleep, but I knew it was a waste of time. If we had a gun in the house, I would have slid it under my pillow. My Louisville Slugger leaning against my bed post would have to do.

"Wake up."

Elijah's voice still lingered in my head when I sat up in bed. Had I dozed off? I cursed my own subconscious, as I was actually getting great sleep. I was about to lay back down when I heard his voice again, but louder this time.

"Go outside."

My phone was on my nightstand, but I decided not to take it. I picked it up to glance at the time. It was only 11:25. Instead, my hands found the baseball bat, and I prepared myself for battle before leaving my bedroom. I hurried down the main hall, out into the living room. Was I dreaming all of this? Maybe I was having one of those night terrors Brandon used to have when he was little.

I smacked myself in the face to make sure this was real.

My imagination decided to play a trick on me, and it started playing the Friday the 13th music in my head. I cursed myself for having watched all of the 80s flicks over the summer while I unlocked the deadbolt and door knob lock. I opened the door, ready to swing at whatever was on the front porch. Only a warm late-August breeze greeted me as I stepped outside.

The street sounded too quiet. Even at eleven o'clock, there was usually a little activity in the neighborhood. At least a stray car would drive by, or a few lights or flashes of TV screens coming through the neighbors' windows somewhere, but my street was pitch black except for the street light. There couldn't have been a power outage. Even the wind seemed silent.

I steadied my grip on my weapon and crept along the side of the house towards the backyard. The damn garden hose nearly tripped me up, and it seemed there was nothing I could do to stop making so much noise with my clumsy footsteps. I'd make a terrible ninja.

When I came to the corner of my house, a loud buzzing in my head made me lose my bearings. My vision spun, and my stomach churned with acid. Whatever lurked in the backyard was causing the interference messing with my brain. Were Level 6 agents back there waiting for me, using their psionic powers to break my will?

I'd seen enough science fiction and action movies to know that either my greatest fear or a helpless cat was just around the corner. We were never a religious family, but I found myself praying before gathering my sad excuse for bravery and jumping out with my bat at the ready.

I let out a ferocious battle cry as I swung around the corner. When a pair of blazing red eyes pierced the darkness, I nearly lost the grip on my bat. The monster's wings folded back behind it's towering body, and the ringing in my ears got so intense, I swore they had to be bleeding by now.

"Get out!" I cocked my arms, ready to send the Mothman's head to left field.

The creature didn't howl, or scream, or even roar. Instead, it hummed. The sound seemed to come from its belly. It was low and had a vibrating quality to it. Was it trying to speak to me?

I'm sorry, dude. I don't speak Mothmanese.

At night, my backyard was utterly dark, but its flaming eyes provided enough light for me to see its massive humanoid shoulders. It had legs, but I couldn't make out anything more than a silhouette. I hoped my retinas were going to be spared from staring at its eyes, and it seemed to know my immediate fear.

The intensity of the fire lowered enough for me to not have to squint.

"What are you?" That was a stupid question, so I had to be more specific. "Why are you here? Are you here to warn us about the landfill? Is something terrible going to happen?"

The Mothman shifted its stance, but it didn't reply in any discernable way.

I was rationalizing everything, so I decided to take Maverick's advice and just let myself feel. Other than absolutely terrified, my gut told me the creature wasn't there to eat me or rip my head off. If it wanted to, I'd already be dead meat. There was a purpose to its presence.

I whispered, "You're here to help."

Its wings ruffled from behind its back. I took that as a "yes." I didn't want to let go of my baseball bat. Against a seven-foot-tall winged monster, I might as well have been holding a foam noodle.

"How can you help me? How can you help us?"

The vibrating growl came from its mouth, if it had an actual mouth. Stretching out its long arm, it held out one hand. The Mothman had only four fingers, and each ended with eagle-like talons that could easily slice and dice me like Wolverine's vibranium claws could. Did it want my bat? Or maybe it wanted me to step closer to it? Both options sucked.

"You want me to come closer?"

Once again, its vocalization most definitely came out of its mouth, but I couldn't tell if it had fangs or teeth. My eyes fully adjusted to the darkness, but for some reason, I couldn't focus too long on its face except for the red orbs glowing, albeit at a lower wattage.

I took three hesitant steps towards it, lowering my bat in the process. The Mothman didn't move, so I guess I wasn't close enough yet. My wobbly legs brought me another three steps closer, despite my rational mind screaming for me to run away.

Its wings blew open like a sail being unfurled on the open seas. Again, I took note of the Mothman's silver feathers. I swore one slipped to the ground, but I wasn't sure. Startled, I jumped back for a moment. If it wanted to, it could have grabbed me with its razor-sharp claws and hurled me up into the sky like a hawk snatching up a field mouse, but it continued to beckon me closer.

"I just turned eighteen. I've lived a pretty good life."

I took a deep breath and moved forward. I stood less than three feet away, and the cloister bells in my head quieted down until the only sound in my backyard was the rustling of the weeping willow tree directly behind the Mothman. Without warning, its red eyes flared as brightly as the sun. I let out a pitiful scream and completely lost my balance.

My butt slammed into the grass, and I knew I was now totally blind for life. All I could see were pulsating, purple orbs in my field of vision. The creature's wings ruffled again, and a swooshing sound told me it had thrust itself up into the air and was probably flying away.

I struggled to stand back up; I was beyond dizzy. In the fourth grade, we had been playing Karate Kid, and Dylan did the crane kick to my head. My head pounded so badly, and I remembered not being able to see anything. This was ten times worse. I stumbled forward, landing on my baseball bat. I reached underneath my belly and grabbed it. Using it as a cane, I pulled myself up and staggered towards what I hoped was the patio table and chairs.

You will be...

I ignored Elijah's voice inside my head. I had bigger problems. Rubbing my eyes would do no good, but at least the purple fireballs dominating my eyesight were starting to fade. I felt for a chair, and I threw myself into it. I did all I could to calm down and control my shallow breathing. I didn't move.

...at the center...

Had my dead brother set a trap for me? A faraway dog barked, and the sound of an angry truck or van rumbled past the house. I put my hand in front of my face, and I could make out my fingers, but my palm was completely blocked by the black splotches still lingering in my vision. Drops of sweat poured from my scalp down my face, stinging my now blind eyes.

...of a great tragedy.

I already felt like the center of a great tragedy. I was now blind. After several long minutes, the blind spots were replaced by fluttering floaters. They looked like amoebas flying around, but at least I could see my hands in front of my face. My heart finally stopped racing, and the wind dried my sweat to cool me down. The sky had changed. A trace of light made it possible to see all the trees around me. Was it moonlight? Where had the moon been all this time?

I'm not sure how long I sat in the chair, but it couldn't have been more than an hour before my eyesight returned to normal. I picked up my baseball bat and made my way back towards the front of the house. When I turned the corner, I just about had another panic attack. A hint of the emerging sun kissed the horizon. Was it morning already?

I had originally come out here at eleven thirty. What the hell?

In a frenzy, I scurried back inside the house. Before going to my bedroom, I stopped in the kitchen to pour myself some orange juice. I gulped it down, and the sugary drink had never tasted so delicious. When I got back to my room, the first thing I did was grab my phone.

It was 5:58 in the morning.

You will be at the center of a great tragedy.
Yeah. No shit.

CHAPTER 18

NO TIME FOR even a power nap.

I stumbled to the shower, inspecting my face in the mirror while letting the water run so it'd warm up. Other than the whites of my eyes being a little bloodshot, I wasn't suffering from corneal or facial sunburn this time. Amazing. I was certain half my face had melted off last night. Or had it happened early this morning?

Alien abductees often talked about lost time after being dropped back on earth, but at least that somewhat made sense. They were often sedated and such. However, I had been totally awake, right? Now, I wasn't so sure anymore. My mind replayed the night's events, and I didn't recall being knocked out. Then again, my video recorder of a mind wouldn't have been recording if I had been unconscious.

I remembered everything. Getting the bat. Even the distinctive smells, sounds, and sensations came back to me. The Mothman spoke, sort of. Or it shook its wings to communicate with me. Wings. Feathers.

Feather!

I shut off the shower and ran straight for the front door. Mom and Dad, thankfully, were still getting ready in their master bath.

The sun hid behind some thick clouds, which made it look earlier than it really was. A car drove by, and a couple joggers were at the end of the street. I hurried around the house, to the backyard. I used the weeping willow tree as my guide to estimate where the Mothman had been standing. I practically dove onto the turf, inspecting it for footprints. Nothing. I moved towards the tree on my hands and knees, and that was when I found a silvery feather.

This thing had to be two feet long. Almost as long as a peacock feather, but it looked like the kind the Founders used to sign the Declaration of Independence, except it was three times the size. With trembling fingers, I picked it up and studied it. It felt like silk, but more rigid. The color was strange. Dark gray towards the tip, but the rest of it was an iridescent silver color.

I'd have to bring it to school and ask my old biology teacher if she could help me identify it. For the hell of it, I sniffed it, and it smelled like nothing. I kept the feather down at my side as I walked back into the house, and Dad greeted me in the living room.

"Out for a jog?" he joked, knowing I wasn't a runner.

I felt my face get hot. "I'm just helping Shannon with a school project by looking for bird feathers." I made sure he didn't see the gargantuan feather behind my back. "I'm going to get a shower. Running late as usual."

Dad nodded and started for the kitchen.

I hurried past him, and without thinking, I blurted out, "Don't take the Rock Road today, Dad."

"Why? Did you hear about an accident on the news or something?"

"Sounded pretty bad," I replied. "You'll get to the office faster taking the back way around."

Dad looked like he was going to turn on the TV to verify, but he shrugged his shoulders and went to the kitchen instead. "Thanks for the heads up."

I had no idea why I had told him to avoid the main road to his work, but it was the little voice inside my head talking to me again. The gut feeling was much stronger this time, though, and there was no ignoring it.

With my super-sized feather in hand, I went straight to my room and put it carefully inside my backpack. I glanced at my phone on the nightstand to check the time, and Shannon had texted me three times and tried to call me twice. The texts were for all four of us.

Get to school early. Meet in the parking lot again!

Brandon and Dylan were already at Shannon's car when I got there. By the looks of it, she had already told them something important, as they all looked weary and stressed out. Dylan appeared as exhausted as ever, but Shannon looked just as bad. Without having to ask, I already knew what had happened.

"You too?" I asked her.

She nodded. "I actually stopped to get a soda. I never do that, but I need the caffeine."

"Welcome to the club," Dylan said with a salute. He turned to me. "Last night, I dreamed about the Cardinals beating the Reds 14-2. The sky was red, and a huge storm leveled the whole city. But there was this old 1940s radio on the ground, all smashed up. The damn thing was still working, and that's when I heard the score. Messed up, huh?"

Brandon shut his eyes tightly. "Oh crap, I'm next. No more dreams about finding a bag of money in my hamper."

We had a great laugh out of that one, although Shannon let out a pitiful sigh.

"We'll figure this out," I told her. "I've got something to cheer you up."

I put my backpack on the ground, unzipped it, and

pulled out the giant feather as if I was unveiling Excalibur from its sheath.

"Holy shit!" Dylan reached up to grab it, and I let him inspect it. "It's ginormous!"

Shannon and Brandon eagerly awaited their turn to hold it.

"I actually spoke to it last night," I said.

Brandon almost dropped our otherworldly evidence. "What?"

I said, "The Mothman was in my backyard, standing under the tree. It didn't speak or anything, but it would let out this weird growl or shake its wings when I asked it questions. I asked if it was here to help, and in its own way, it said yes. Then it wanted me to come closer, which I did."

"You're friggin' crazy," Shannon said. "Did you get a better look at it this time?"

"Yeah. It's for sure super tall. Maybe seven feet tall. It lowered the brightness of its eyes for a moment, just so I could actually look at it better. It has a head, but I couldn't tell the shape because of the massive neck and shoulder muscles making it look like the Hulk. It was all hunchbacky and stuff. It had big-ass claws, though. Four fingers. I couldn't make out its legs, but there's two legs for sure. I didn't see actual feet."

Shannon caressed the feather. "And it's got feathers. Big ones."

I asked them, "Should we take it to Mrs. Lee? Maybe she can help eliminate all the normal possibilities."

"That's a great idea," Dylan said.

Brandon said, "If she can't identify it, though, you think she'll call the zoo or something? Then your discovery will be made public, probably. You'd have news vans at your house asking questions."

"It's just a damn feather," I said.

"No, it's not!" Shannon waved it around my face. "Brandon's right. Mrs. Lee might ask a zoologist or somebody to take a look at it. Then you're going to find yourself in the spotlight."

I forced my mind to stop racing with possibilities and allow myself to just quiet my thoughts. "I think bringing it to Mrs. Lee is the right thing to do. I just have a feeling."

With a shrug, Shannon handed it to me, and I put it back into my backpack. Before we could head to the school's main entrance, Mr. Sullivan, the tenth-grade principal came up behind us with his walkie talkie blaring.

"I'm glad you guys missed the accident," Mr. Sullivan said.

"What accident?" Shannon asked him.

He turned down the volume so we could hear him. "There's a five-car pileup on the Rock Road that happened just five minutes ago. I hope none of the students or teachers are involved, but I get a feeling a large percentage of folks are going to be late to first hour this morning."

Mr. Sullivan hurried past us and entered through the lobby doors.

My mouth went dry.

"What's wrong with you, Jonah?" Shannon examined my face like a doctor would. "You OK?"

I pulled my phone out of my pocket to check on Dad, but he sent me a text already.

It read, "Heard there was another bad accident on Rock Road. Took the back way into work. Are you OK?"

The others crowded around me to read Dad's message.

"I told him to avoid Rock Road this morning," I explained to them.

Brandon remarked, "Good thinking."

"But I told him an hour ago," I whispered.

Shannon grabbed me by the shoulder. "That's crazy."

Dylan rubbed his forehead. "Are we all going to be able to predict the future too?"

"I hope," Shannon said as she led the way to the lobby doors. "I need to predict some lottery ticket numbers. "

"You're not eighteen yet," Brandon said with a chuckle.

"Jonah is." Shannon slapped my back. "If you're going to be predicting the future, you might as well get rich off of it, right?"

My gut told me there would be no glory or riches to come from this "gift." It was a burden placed on my shoulders, and now I had to figure out what the hell to do with it. I had already seen the future, and there was only death.

Mrs. Lee's planning hour was third period, so I went to her classroom after my second class. She was at her desk grading papers when I walked in. She gave me a big smile as she stood up. Mrs. Lee had been my Biology 1 and 2 teacher, and she had tried to talk me into being a surgeon. Apparently, I was amazing at dissecting stuff.

I explained I had found a feather in my backyard, and I needed her help identifying it. She agreed, and when I slid it out of my backpack, her mouth dropped open.

"Whoa." Mrs. Lee took hold of the feather and stared at it for a good two minutes before saying, "I think you might have totally stumped me, Mr. Ashe. I've never seen anything like this. You got this from your backyard?"

I nodded. "The coloring is weird."

"It's shimmering, like a peacock feather," she noted. "And from the shape, it's definitely a primary feather."

"Primary?" My knowledge of birds was pretty much nonexistent.

"It's the outer feathers of a bird's wing, and they're the biggest ones. They're the ones responsible for a thrust in flight." Her free hand stroked the feather from tip to tip. "The shape, color, and size completely throw me off." She turned her attention to me. "You want me to ask some colleagues of mine? I don't know any ornithologists, but I have friends who could find one for me."

Brandon was right, but my inner voice told me to let her talk to an expert. "Sure."

Mrs. Lee went back to studying the feather. "This could be a very significant find." She elbowed me jokingly. "Don't worry, I won't steal your discovery."

"That's the least of my worries."

CHAPTER 19

AT LUNCH, SHANNON had been quieter than usual. I knew exactly what she was going through. I wasn't sure if I should ask her about her dream. Slowly, she revealed to me what had happened. Many of the same elements of Dylan and my visions were there—all the death and destruction was all around her. The message she received, however, was more specific. In Dylan's dreams, he was told she would need him. In mine, I heard he would need me.

Shannon was told by a faraway voice she swore was mine that I was the one who would need her on the tragic day to come.

The parking lot after school was already half empty by the time Brandon met us by my car. He wasn't much of a runner, but I had never seen him sprinting so fast in my life. He practically busted through the lobby doors, and we were afraid he might get hit by a car. When he reached us, he was sucking wind.

"What is it?" Dylan asked him.

Brandon folded his hands behind his head. "The net has blown up."

Shannon got out her own phone. "The UFO Network?"

"Yup, and just about every other social media site and message board," Brandon replied. People are not only reporting UFOs, but there's been six witnesses who saw a flying man in the sky in Bridgetowne and Maryville Heights."

There was some comfort in not feeling so alone. "It's spreading," I said.

"Like a cancer," Dylan remarked. "The whole town is going crazy."

"Not any crazier than us." Shannon kept messing with her phone. "On the Network, one person even mentioned the landfill."

I jingled my keys. "You guys still up for staking it out and getting the Mothman on video? Show people they aren't hallucinating. Maybe we can all figure this thing out together."

The other three nodded, but I couldn't shake a vague, sinking feeling. The moment I opened my car door, I heard my inner voice loud and clear. "Dylan, can you drive?"

"I'm parked way over by the football stadium," he

whined.

I shut my door and put my keys inside my pocket.

"Is your Spidey sense tingling?" Shannon asked me.

"Yeah."

A deep crease formed between Brandon's eyes. "Is your car going to break down or something?"

"I don't think that's it," I answered. "I just know I'm not supposed to drive."

Dylan opened his backpack to search for his keys. "You've been pretty accurate so far, Nostradamus. We might as well keep listening to your prophecies."

I knew something significant was going to happen at the landfill today, something bad. There was no escaping it. My rational brain told me to avoid fate by changing our plans and just going home. Deep down, I knew whether I went home or whether I flew to Australia, destiny was going to chase me down and beat me over the head.

A small crowd had congregated just outside the landfill's main gate. At first, we thought they were protesters, but none of them were holding signs or chanting "Clean it up!" Dylan parked his truck at my dad's office, and we walked across the street to where the others were gathered. Instead of holding picket signs, they carried cameras, many with large telescoping lenses.

"Looks like they had the same idea," I said.

We hung back but eavesdropped on a middle-aged lady talking to a younger guy with a professional-looking camera. She was talking fast, as if she needed to spit out her words quickly so she wouldn't forget them. The camera man kept nodding his head, listening intently to her rapid-fire speaking.

"My husband has terrible eyesight for reading, but he can see out in the distance just fine," she told him. "What does that mean? Is he nearsighted or farsighted?"

"Farsighted," the camera man replied.

"His car is in the shop. Bad alternator. I had to pick him up after work last night around ten. He works at the Masco warehouse a block away. He was already out, waiting for me, smoking. He thought maybe it was just a bat flying over the landfill, but when he got a better look, he said it was way too big to be a damn bat. He ran over here to get a better look, and sure enough, the flying creature flew right over his head, maybe fifty feet up."

The camera man asked her, "What did he say it looked like?"

"Huge wingspan. He guessed ten feet. Grayish in color. But its eyes terrified him. The creature's eyes were glowing red. It hurt him to even look at its eyes from far away."

"Did you see it?"

The lady shook her head. "It was already gone when I got here."

Brandon looked like he wanted to burst, so we dragged him away from the scene.

I whispered, "I'm not ready to start talking about meeting the Mothman to anyone else."

Brandon said, "What if others have had a close encounter like yours? If no one comes forward, you'll all think you're alone in all this. Maybe you're not."

"I'm not going to assume I'm special," I said. "I get the feeling the Mothman has gotten up close and personal with other people too, but I'm not ready to get a bunch of cameras thrown in my face. My parents would freak. I'd get hauled away to the psych ward for sure."

Dylan said, "With all of this new attention, maybe the evidence will make it easier for others to come forward with their stories. It has to get to a certain point where we just can't ignore it any more. What if somebody credible, like the mayor or a police officer, were to come forward with their testimony? Then you won't seem nearly as crazy."

"Who's going to believe a high school kid?" I glanced at the group of fellow truth-seekers. "You're right, it would help if others came forward too. Credible witnesses."

Brandon checked his phone. "We've got three hours until dark. Being out here so early is a waste of time. It seems the Mothman only likes to come out at night."

"Not cliché at all," Shannon said with a smirk.

Several of those with big cameras started snapping pictures up in the sky, but they let out a collective groan when they realized it was just a big hawk.

Out of habit, I glanced at my own phone to confirm it was only 3:32. "We can't assume."

The young guy with the huge lens kept his camera pointed upwards. "I see something!"

He pointed high above the landfill, up towards the clouds. We all tried to figure out what he was seeing, but I only saw a plane coming in for a landing since the airport was only a couple miles away from here. Shannon squinted her eyes and tugged at my sleeve.

"He's right," she said. "There's something just below the clouds."

"The plane?" Dylan asked.

Shannon pointed upwards. "No. Look to the left of where the plane is, and then go up."

A tiny silver object hovered just below the wispy clouds. It wasn't the Mothman. In fact, I was sure it wasn't organic. It was my very first legit UFO sighting ever in my life. My heart raced, and all I could do was stare and point. Shannon's mouth drew open, Dylan let out a wow, but Brandon still hadn't seen it yet.

By the sounds coming from the crowd, they too were seeing the triangular object floating in the sky. It reflected the sun as if it was made of metal. I wished I had a pair of binoculars with me. The group by the gate snapped away with their cameras.

"I got some great shots," the young guy exclaimed.

"That doesn't look like a flying monster," the lady said. "Looks like a spaceship."

I blinked, and the UFO shot up into the clouds.

Another guy with a video camera yelled, "Damn! Did you see that? I totally captured it."

I was so excited, I hadn't noticed Shannon tapping my shoulder from behind. When I swiveled around to her, she looked as if she might cry.

"Level 6 is here," she said through tight lips.

Without being too obvious, I surveyed the area. Sure enough, the two men in dark blue suits stood next to Dylan's truck across the street. As always, both wore sunglasses, while only one wore the gangster fedora.

"What do we do?" Brandon asked the group.

I swallowed the lump in my throat and replied, "Let's go have a chat with our Men in Black."

"You guys have great timing," I said to them as we approached Dylan's truck.

Neither man's expression changed. My head filled with static, and from the scrunched-up faces of the others, they were feeling it too. This was part of their mind-controlling, and we had to remain vigilant to resist it.

"So, if you were to ask us, now, if we've seen any strange things in the sky, we'd have to say yes," I continued. "And those people near the gate got it on film. Maybe you should be hassling them now, right?"

The man with the black hair stepped towards us. Brandon retreated a bit, but the rest of us didn't budge. "We're not interested in them."

I didn't know how to respond, so I kept my mouth shut.

"I'm sure Maverick Ashe told you all about us," the black-haired agent said. "His point of view is quite subjective, though. Tainted."

Maverick had told me to play dumb, but there was no fooling these guys. "Can you really blame him?"

Shannon stepped toward the black-haired man's face. "What do you want?"

Fedora guy pointed at me.

"No way," Shannon said in almost a growl.

In an even and cool tone, the black-haired agent said, "Please come with us, Jonah. We promise no harm will come to you. We just need to ask you some questions."

"Yeah right." Dylan went to Shannon's side. "This

is America, buddy. You can't just rip some guy off the street and start torturing him and stuff."

"Torture?" Fedora guy moved away from his car and took off his hat. He too had jet black hair slicked back, just like his partner. "No. No torture. Just a discussion. Maybe you'll learn more about what's happening to you, what's happening to all of you, if you just come with us for a little bit. We promise to have you back at your car you left at Monument High by six o'clock."

I walked past Shannon and Dylan, and they both grabbed me by the shoulders. "I'm good." I wiggled out of their clutches. "I'll call you guys after we're done."

"Don't do it!" Brandon reached out to pull me back. "Their mind control is working on you, Jonah."

"It's not. I know what I'm doing."

Shannon was on the verge of totally losing it. "I don't like this one bit."

I whispered to her, "I knew this was going to happen." I turned to the Level 6 agents. "After I cooperate, you promise to leave my friends alone?"

"Yes," the agent said before putting his hat back on his head. "If you fully cooperate, we will leave you all alone."

The black-haired guy went back to the car and opened one of the rear doors. "Your cousin told you some half-truths about us. If we wanted to harm any of you, we would have done it a long time ago."

I pulled away from the others and got into the black Mercedes. "Don't tell my parents," I said to them before the door shut behind me.

The leather was warm, and the interior of the car smelled brand new. The black-haired agent got back behind the wheel. Fedora guy took his seat next to him.

"We appreciate your cooperation," Fedora guy said.

Shannon, Dylan, and Brandon stood like statues next to the truck as they watched us drive away. The Mercedes made a U-turn in the parking lot before making a right turn on the industrial road leading to Rock Road. I waved at them from the passenger window, and I forced a smile on my face.

I prayed it wasn't the last time I'd ever see my friends.

CHAPTER 20

I WASN'T TOO familiar with the actual city of St. Louis, like many suburbanites, but I knew we were heading towards the old industrial part of town. Not too far away, I could see the Gateway Arch in the distance. During the entire thirty-minute car ride, neither agent spoke a word. It was a relief when the static in my head disappeared, but it took all of my power to keep the terror inside my chest in check. I had taken my cell phone out a couple of times, but I noticed I had no service at all. That didn't surprise me. Instead, I just kept staring out of the window in an effort to calm myself. We came to an old factory building with a fenced parking lot. Our car stopped at the machine-operated gate for a moment before it let us in.

The parking lot was only half-filled with cars, and the Mercedes finally came to a stop in a lonely parking space away from the congregation of abandoned vehicles near the door. Both men got out, and the guy with the fedora opened the door for me. I stepped out and followed them.

It had been too quiet for too long, so I asked them, "Is this your secret lair?"

"Not really a secret," the agent with the black hair replied. "Otherwise, we would have blindfolded you."

We walked up a flight of old stairs. The ancient, crumbled brick walls surrounded us. A stale, metallic stench made me gag. Whatever used to be manufactured here had something to do with burning metal. Fedora guy led us up another two floors, while the black-haired one trailed behind me.

"Can you at least tell me your names?" My legs felt heavy, and I was starting to suck wind. "It would help make all of this less creepy."

"Perkins," Fedora guy answered.

The black-haired agent didn't reply right away. When we got to our floor, he said, "My name is Stewart."

A yellowish glow from antique fluorescent lights flooded the decaying corridor. Agent Perkins went to one of five doors on this floor and opened it. He removed his hat and pointed to the three chairs in the empty lobby. "Just take a seat. When he's ready for you, he'll open his office door."

Agent Stewart started to shut the door behind him. "We'll be right outside."

I was about to ask him who I was meeting with, but

I decided not to. The chairs looked like they were from the 70s. Dusty, maroon fabric covered the cushions, and the metal legs looked rusted. Level 6 might be a top-secret government organization, but they were on a tight budget.

After brushing some of the dirt off the chairs, I sat down. The seat was even more uncomfortable than it looked. Out of curiosity, I glanced at my phone, but it remained useless. I only had to wait a couple of minutes before the office door opened, and a Eurasian-looking guy stepped out wearing a dress shirt and slacks.

"Hi Jonah. I'm Dr. Park."

He didn't offer his hand for me to shake, but he did actually give me a genuine smile. Dr. Park left the door open for me, so I stepped through into his large office. The windows overlooked the street below, and a lot of natural light flooded the open space. A modern desk sat right in the middle of the room with two leather chairs scooted right up against it. He motioned for me to take a seat. On the opposite wall was a flat-screen television, which looked so out of place in this ragged, abandoned building. It was amazing this place still had electricity.

Dr. Park walked behind his desk, which only had a desk lamp, a steno notebook opened to a blank page, and a fancy looking pen. I was a little hungry, but I assumed getting a snack wasn't going to happen here.

"Thank you for agreeing to come here," he said as he sat down.

I decided to start with some small talk. "Park. That's Korean, right?"

"Yes. My grandparents immigrated from Korea. My mom is English and Irish." Dr. Park picked up his pen and started spinning it in his long fingers. "Maybe if we had more time, we could have an interesting discussion on what it's like to be a half-Asian American, but you know why we're here."

I had to keep playing dumb. "Your agents have been asking us about seeing UFOs, and we actually did today. It was pretty amazing. Perkins and Stewart were there."

Dr. Park wasn't buying it. "There has been an increase in UFO activity in St. Louis, particularly in Bridgetowne. But that's not the real reason why we're meeting today."

"I have no idea what you're talking about," I shot back.

"Maverick probably told you to play innocent with us, but you and I are actually on the same team," Dr. Park said. "I can't blame him for hating us. It's understandable as to why your cousin would see us as the enemy."

I wasn't going to give this guy anything.

"Just like any large bureaucracy, there's good and bad," Dr. Park continued, "and there's everything in between. Level 6's job is very simple. Protect society."

I couldn't stop myself from spitting some venom, but Dr. Park was starting to really piss me off. "Protect it from the truth, you mean."

Dr. Park nodded. "Oftentimes, protecting the public from the truth is necessary. Could you imagine what would have happened in the 1950s had we fully disclosed everything we knew about alien life? America would have descended into absolute anarchy. Between all the UFO hunters and conspiracy theorists out there leaking accurate information for the last sixty years, the public is now better prepared to handle the truth. It's all about timing. We protect society from itself."

"By any means necessary?"

"Sometimes." Dr. Park looked like he was going to write something, but he stopped himself. "What can you tell me about the flying creature?"

My head started to throb the moment I heard the static in my head. This guy was trying to pull his mind control crap on me, but I wasn't going to let him. Instead, I decided to focus on the most traumatic day of my life. It would be my defense against his will-bending powers.

"The safety of your community is at stake," Dr. Park said. "Bigger picture, the entire region is in danger." He pulled open a drawer, and I prepared myself for him to pull a gun on me. Instead, he got out a file folder. Inside were pictures, which he slid over to me. "Take a look at them. Notice anything they have in common?"

The first picture looked to be like a teenage girl with freckles. Another was of an older man with a mustache. The third photograph was of a young black kid with a wide grin. I pulled a picture of a Hispanic boy from underneath the pile.

"I don't see what any of these people have in common," I replied. "Different races. Ages. Genders. They're all different."

Dr. Park reached over and put the pictures back into the folder. "It's a very diverse group, on the surface. They all have a couple things in common, however. Number one, they all have extraordinary autobiographic memories. They all have hyperthymesia, just like you."

My left eye twitched, and the static continued to grow louder in my ears.

"Just like many who have hyperthymesia, all of these people suffer from depression." Dr. Park placed the folder back into his drawer as if he was handling a velvet bag of diamonds. "It must be difficult for you to be able to recall, in such vivid detail, your most horrible experiences. Sure, you can relive your greatest days too, but it's the tragic ones that haunt you."

This guy was playing psychological games with me, which made me even angrier. "What else do all of those people have in common?"

"They've all had a personal encounter with a being many call The Mothman." Dr. Park's eyes remained fixated on my face, as if he was trying to detect any kind of physical reaction from me. "I believe you too have had such an encounter."

The man who had grabbed Elijah was wearing a red shirt and white shorts. He stood under six-feet tall. His sandy blond hair was long and wispy, and it was thin on the crown. He had brown eyes and high cheekbones. The man had a tattoo of a bird on his left forearm, and the back of his neck bore a large brown mole. Brian K. Morris kidnapped, molested, and killed my brother.

"Tell me about the Mothman, Elijah."

I snapped. "Stop fucking with me! You think by calling me by my brother's name, I'm going to break down and tell you everything? You can forget it. Kiss my ass. I'm done here!"

I stood up, and Dr. Park's easygoing demeanor evaporated. I thought my mind might be playing tricks on me, but the whites of his eyes disappeared. His eyes had become big black pools, as if his soul had been suddenly ripped from his body. The devil himself stood in front of me.

Dr. Park's voice echoed in my head. *Sit down.*

My instincts told me something bad was going to happen if I didn't follow his orders, so I took my seat. The static in my head dissipated, but I still felt like he was doing something to my mind. Instead of pushing his control over me, he was trying to pull my mental energy away. It was as if Dr. Park had the ability to drain the fight out of me.

I blinked several times, thinking my vision and Dr. Park's eyes would return to normal, but it was no use. His eyes were as black as night, and the source of his dark power seemed to emanate from them.

"I have more pictures." Dr. Park pulled the same drawer and produced a green folder. He opened it and flashed photos of yet another set of diverse people. "These folks don't have hyperthymesia. However, they do suffer from OCD."

I kept trying to pull my gaze away from his black eyes, but I couldn't. "Obsessive Compulsive Disorder."

"Do you know what a SPECT scan is, Jonah?" Dr. Park asked me calmly.

I shook my head.

"It's special imaging technology. It can record the areas of your brain firing up. A person who is recalling a pleasant memory is typically going to have a different SPECT scan compared to someone, say, sleeping." Dr. Park shoved the pictures back into the folder and put them in his desk. "Interestingly, the SPECT scan of someone with hyperthymesia is very similar to a person with OCD. People with OCD have an astronomically higher rate of reporting an encounter with the Mothman."

My will to keep fighting his mind-push subsided with my revelation that others like me had run into the Mothman. "Did they get corneal sunburn too?"

Dr. Park thought for a moment. "Actually, yes. Most of them did. A few had blood vessels in their eyes burst. You haven't just come face-to-face with this mysterious creature once, have you? You saw it again very recently."

How did he know all this? I could understand him knowing I had gone to the ophthalmologist when my corneas got fried. But with my latest encounter in my yard, there's no way he could have known unless he was there. Did he know about the feather? Again, I felt a mental tugging in my head. Was he yanking information from my brain?

I crossed my arms and imagined psychically pushing him out of my head. "I don't like you mentally molesting me. If you want me to talk, you need to cut it out."

Dr. Park put his hand to his chin for a long moment, and the blackness in his eyes dissolved. My muscles eased a bit, and I took a deep inhale of stale air before pushing it out of my lungs. The room turned colder, and the static in my head remained absent.

"Is that better?" he asked me.

"Much." I leaned back in my seat. "I had a recent sighting, yes. Just last night. The Mothman was in my backyard, and it did something to me."

Dr. Park started scribbling notes on his notepad. "What do you mean? Did he touch or hurt you?"

"No. His red eyes exploded, completely blinding me. I couldn't see for a really long time." Despite the cooler air in the room, a drop of cold sweat ran down my cheek. "The whole incident took maybe fifteen, twenty minutes. When my eyesight went back to normal and I went back inside to look at my phone, more than six hours had passed."

After he finished writing, he looked up at me. "Have you felt differently since then? Like something's somehow off?"

I knew it was no use trying to hide anything from this guy. "Ever since my first encounter, I've been having strange dreams. I've also been passing out randomly. The strangest thing is, I've been able to sense events before they happen."

"Precognition?" Dr. Park went back to writing. "Can you give me an example?"

"This morning, I told my dad not to take his usual route to work. I lied and said there was something about a traffic jam. I just knew he should stay off Rock Road. Sure enough, there was a horrible accident there. He would have been in the middle of it."

Dr. Park asked me, "You said you just knew it. Can you describe that kind of knowing?"

"It's a strong emotion, the kind I can't ignore," I replied. "There's a voice telling me things, but it's not really a voice using actual words. It uses strong emotions to get my attention and convey to me all sorts of things about to happen. I don't get mental pictures, though. It's hard to explain."

I waited for him to stop writing before I asked him, "Are the others in your files having similar experiences?"

Dr. Park put his pen down. "So far, I've spoken to twenty-nine people with their own stories to tell. There are elements that are similar. Out of twenty-nine, only six have described suddenly having the ability to predict future events. Including you, that makes seven."

He was leveling with me, which was a good sign. I decided to go for broke. "What can you tell me about the Mothman?"

"I assume you did a little research about Point Pleasant, West Virginia. 1967. Silver Bridge collapse and all?"

"Yeah. Many believe the Mothman came as a sort of omen of the bridge collapsing."

After swiveling in his chair to face away from me, Dr. Park said, "The government took special interest in the Point Pleasant case, and an organization I consider to be the forefather of our own group investigated the Mothman sightings. There have been just a handful of other cases we have examined. 1986, the Chernobyl nuclear plant disaster. 2001, September 11th. 2007, the collapse of the I-35 bridge in Minneapolis. 2009, the swine flu outbreak in La Junta, Mexico."

"Are you telling me, the Mothman was seen flying around just prior to all of these disasters? 9/11 too? I read something about that, but I didn't believe it." My face felt hot to the touch. "Where does this thing come from?"

Dr. Park swung back around to face me. "We've been studying the Mothman phenomenon for over fifty years, and we're not much closer to solving the mystery than we were in 1967. What we do know is this: it appears prior to a major catastrophic event. From the eyewitness testimonies, it seems to single out people who suffer from OCD or hyperthymesia. Why? We don't know for sure. We can only hypothesize it has to do with the way your brains work. For a select few individuals like yourself, the Mothman is associated with triggering extra sensory perception, particularly precognition. One-hundred percent of these poor souls have had their lives turned upside down. I imagine you too are suffering."

I didn't want to give Dr. Park the pleasure of knowing he had gained my trust, so I tried to keep my face as expressionless as possible. "It hasn't been easy."

"The origin of the Mothman remains unknown," Dr. Park said. "Some say it's a fallen angel of some kind, sent here to warn us of impending dangers. Others believe it's a creature from a different dimension."

Now I fully understood the term mind-blown. "What does all this UFO activity have to do with the Mothman?"

"We are uncertain," was all Dr. Park said.

It was obvious he was keeping a lot from me, but he had given me some new insight. "If something terrible is going to happen here in St. Louis, why can't you order an evacuation or something? People are going to die."

"We live in a chaotic world, but we pretend that everything has a rational explanation, Jonah. What should we tell the governor? I have testimony of thirty people who've been visited by a flying creature, and they swear some kind of disaster is about to descend on St. Louis?"

He was telling more lies. If he wanted to, he could get the city to evacuate. "What do you want me to do now?"

Dr. Park opened a different drawer and took out a very generic-looking phone. He placed it on his wooden desk and pushed it towards me. "The next time you have a one-on-one with the Mothman, call me. Or if you have another nightmare or vision with something more specific, more definite warning sign of an impending disaster, let me know."

"Are you here to save lives?" I asked Dr. Park.

"Of course, Jonah."

Total lie.

I stared at the new phone for a few seconds before picking it up. "You want something specific?"

"Yes."

I stood up and slid the new phone in my other pocket. "The Cardinals will beat the Reds 14-2."

CHAPTER 21

THIRTY MINUTES LATER, Agents Stewart and Perkins dropped me off at the school parking lot. Without saying a word, they waited for me to open my own door and step out. Shannon, Brandon, and Dylan had been waiting by my car, and they rushed towards me after the agents zoomed away.

"Are you OK?" Shannon asked me.

"I'm fine."

Brandon grabbed me by the shoulder. "I literally freaked out after you left."

"Aw, thanks for your concern, Brandon."

"No, we saw three more UFOs!" Brandon handed me his phone, and sure enough he had snapped pictures of three more triangular black objects. "By the time we left the landfill, there had to be at least twenty people getting footage with all their cameras and stuff. It was nuts."

Dylan looked as if he might fall over from exhaustion. "What happened, man?"

I glanced at my phone. I had been in the custody of Level 6 for almost exactly two hours. It was just starting to get dark, and my stomach growled. "I'll tell you everything, but I'm starving."

Shannon's eyes widened. "Chinese buffet?"

I jingled my keys, and we all climbed into my car.

I spent a good hour explaining my strange meeting with Dr. Park, making sure to go into detail about how his eyes became completely black and how he had the ability to somehow lower my will to fight him. I showed them the phone he had given me, and I talked about all the other photographs of people who had their own Mothman story to tell.

"Oh great," Dylan dropped his crab Rangoon. "We're all screwed. All four of us are OCD in our own ways."

Shannon slapped the back of Dylan's head. "Speak for yourself. I'm the only normal one here."

Brandon turned pale. "That Dr. Park guy is just like one of those Black-Eyed Kids."

"What the hell is a Black-Eyed Kid?" I was stuffed, yet I finished my General Tso's chicken. "On second thought, forget it. Maybe it's better I don't know. I can only deal with one cryptid at a time."

Shannon tried to be positive. "At least we know for sure we're not totally crazy. There's others out there."

I spun the Level 6 cell phone on our table. "These guys are seriously into mind games." I turned to Brandon and jabbed him with my elbow. "Literally. Even if they didn't have the ability to mess with our minds, they're creepy as hell. And Dr. Park is a liar. He lies like a rug. Level 6 isn't here to prevent a disaster. They're not here to help save lives. We're just one big damn petri dish to them. They'd love to capture the Mothman and dissect his ass."

"Or maybe weaponize him," Dylan whispered.

I said, "Maverick said there are all kinds of Dark Projects going on, experiments on children even, all for the sake of national security. They've been chasing after the Mothman for over fifty years, and they still don't know a damn thing about it. Not anymore than we know, anyway."

"Will you actually call them?" Shannon asked.

Without answering her, I picked up the phone and stared at it for a long time. It was turned off, but I had the feeling it being powered down didn't matter. Level 6 still knew exactly where I was.

"I don't know," I finally answered. "What do you guys think?"

"I would," Brandon said. "If Dr. Park can read your mind, he'll know if you saw the Mothman and didn't call him. That could be bad news."

Shannon shook her head. "Hell no, I wouldn't call. You can't trust those idiots."

I looked at Dylan, and he looked as torn as me. He eventually said, "Brandon is onto something. If they know you didn't report in like they told you to, you might be making an enemy for life. Or worse. Your cousin said they were responsible for his mother and several of his friends' deaths. And a year later, the agents are still following him, just to mess with him."

Shannon touched my hand. "What will you do?"

"I'm not sure," I said. "I guess I'll just have to wait and see what feels right when the time comes."

That night, I stared at a section of my mirror that wasn't foggy after taking a hot shower. My eyes still had dark circles around them, and my cheeks were unusually red. My hair was getting a little out of control, and I'd have to get it cut soon. Would Elijah have grown his hair long too? Or maybe he would have rebelled at how Mom always tried to get us to look exactly the same and have gotten a crew cut. Even in nine short years, he had been the one to question authority any chance he had.

All I wanted right now was to get a good night's sleep. Just one damn night without any visions or nightmares would go a long way towards putting more gas in my tank. Staying awake during the day was such a challenge, I felt like I was having an out-of-body experience every class period. I was only partially present. This was a recipe for disaster, and I tended to make horrible decisions when I was exhausted.

Elijah.

I raised my hand, just to confirm my reflection in the mirror was real. For just a split second, it felt out of sync. That voice in my head. My voice? No. It was Elijah's.

Elijah. Elijah. Elijah. Elijah. Elijah. Elijah.

In the bottom-left corner of the mirror was my brother's name, written in the condensation. Had I written it during a moment of a thick brain fog episode? It could have been me, since I am left-handed. Although it seemed silly, I studied my image and made subtle movements. Sure enough, my reflection was my own. My imagination had gotten the best of me. Who else could have written Elijah on the mirror? I was embarrassed for thinking for even one millisecond that my reflection had done it.

But if I had scribbled my brother's name, why didn't I remember doing it?

I was losing my mind.

"I guess it's my turn," Brandon said.

We had a good fifteen minutes before the warning bell, but the parking lot was already buzzing with cars. I had such an amazing night's sleep, I vowed never to take such a thing for granted ever again. The others, however, were miserable. Dylan had gotten himself a huge Mountain Dew, and Shannon looked disheveled. Brandon had been initiated with his very first apocalyptic nightmare.

He described a storm and a tornado. The ground shook while he ran down his street, tripping over dead bodies. His Aunt Bethany, who had died just last year after a bout with cervical cancer, was in his dream. Just before he woke up, she told him: She will need you.

"And then Aunt Bethany literally held up a sign that said Cardinals beat the Reds 14-2." Brandon looked as if he might cry. "Man, I hope the Mothman doesn't come to my house."

Dylan put his hand on Brandon's shoulder. "It's not a given, Brandon. The Mothman didn't visit my house, or Shannon's."

Shannon was busy doing something with her phone. Without looking up, she said, "I haven't had the pleasure, yet."

She seemed frustrated. Her eyes narrowed, and her fingers flew around her phone's screen. The three of us watched her as she furiously worked her phone.

"Something wrong?" I asked her.

"My phone has been acting weird. Touch screen isn't reacting like it should." She restarted it, and her face turned sour is if her tongue had touched a lemon. "OK, it's working now. Guess who the Cardinals are playing?"

I immediately felt faint. "The Cubs?"

Shannon slapped my arm. "Three game series with the Reds."

Dylan and Brandon had a big test tomorrow, and their exhaustion added to their stress. Shannon was babysitting a neighbor's kid after school. Today, staking out the Mothman was out for all of them. I decided to go on my own.

I wasn't alone after all. A large group of people surrounded the landfill's main gate. I lost count at forty-two, and all of them carried cameras and binoculars. Word had spread quickly. At least there was no sign of Level 6 agents anywhere. I took out their cell phone, and it was powered on. I'm pretty sure I had turned it off. This would have normally struck me as being strange, and maybe throwing this phone would have been the smart thing to do. I pushed it back into my pocket, as I didn't want to feel the wrath of Dr. Park and his freaky black eyes.

After an hour of listening to all the UFO hunters

talking about recent sightings, I decided to leave. Instead of going back to my car, I crossed the street and went towards Dad's work. His car was still in the parking lot, so I walked inside and asked Laurie up front to see him.

"This is an unexpected surprise," Dad said as he entered the lobby. "Is there another protest out there?"

"Worse. It's UFO hunters," I replied.

Dad's eyebrows raised. "Ah. They've been increasing in numbers the last two days. I guess they think aliens are interested in garbage."

"Or radioactive waste."

"That might be it." Dad looked like he wanted to say something, but not in front of Laurie at her desk. "I'm done with my work for today. How about we catch some dinner? Your mother is showing a house at six-thirty, so she said to go ahead and eat on our own. You game?"

I can't remember the last time Dad and I had a meal together, just the two of us. "Yeah. Sounds good. Maybe not barbecue this time, though."

I had a craving for pizza, so Dad drove me to Irma's. I could tell he was a little anxious, as if he was getting ready to have one of his rare "serious talk" moments. The last time we sat down like this, it was right after I had gotten my driver's license. He talked about responsibility and being safe, although he didn't feel compelled to monitor my every move. I'm sure Mom wanted to track me, though. Thank God common sense prevailed.

"How are you doing?" Dad finally came out and asked. "I know you're dealing with a lot right now, but I just want to make sure you're doing alright. I'm hoping you had a good session with Ms. Kim, and you have your appointment with a new doctor on Friday."

I pulled a square piece of pizza from the large pan. "I'm hanging in there."

"When you passed out at Pop's, you really had us worried," Dad said. "I knew your eighteenth birthday was going to be especially difficult."

"It has been," I said.

Dad said, "Did you know your mother still cries at night?"

I nearly choked on my food. "I had no idea."

"We could never fully understand the profound pain you've felt." Dad bit his quivering lower lip. "It is just as difficult for a parent to lose a child. It's horrible, and it feels unnatural to outlive your own child."

Dad and I had talked about Elijah's death a few times, but this was the first time he was really opening up to me about what he and Mom were going through. They had always focused on my well-being, and I had never really stopped to give enough thought as to what kind of hell they've been going through for the last nine years.

I wanted to tell him everything, but it would have made him worry even more about me. Mom would totally freak out for sure too. "With my hyperthymesia, I relive that day over and over again. Down to every single detail. It makes it even harder."

"I understand." Dad finished off his drink. "None of us will ever be the same. But I just want you to know your mother and I don't want to put any pressure on you to work it all out. In fact, you will probably struggle with this for the rest of your life, especially with your autobiographical memory. Sometimes, ignorance is bliss."

The guilt I had been lugging around since I was nine years old had seemed to grow heavier with each passing year. Knowing the way Mom was, I couldn't even imagine the kind of self-blame she was going through. The very thought of it took my breath away.

"I appreciate it, Dad," I told him. "Do you ever think about Brian K. Morris?"

Dad's already pale face blanched. "I try not to, Jonah."

"I do. I was there. I saw him following Elijah into the woods." My chest felt heavy. "If I could kill him with my bare hands, I would."

"He's already dead." The color returned to Dad's

face. His cheeks flushed. "As parents, our job is to protect our children. For a long time, my anger burned just as brightly as yours, but I couldn't live like that." His right hand trembled as it touched his plastic cup. "It might have destroyed my relationship with your mother."

I had much more fury to unload, but I had to cut Dad loose. "I think seeing the new doctor is going to help me. I understand what you're saying. The stress of all of these real-world decisions isn't helping."

"You'll be going away to college soon," Dad said. "You'll be entering a wonderful time in your life when you get to discover who you really are. You've worked hard to give yourself options, and your mother might push here and there because she cares. Just know you have to look inside yourself for those answers. Only you can figure out who you are."

Dad was really pouring his heart out. He never did this much talking. "Got it."

"I hope so." Dad patted my shoulder. "You're on your own timeline. No rush."

If guilt was my straightjacket, then anger was my prison. Brian K. Morris had killed himself when the police were closing in on him. Years later, I came to believe the bastard had robbed us yet again. Justice had not even come close to being served. I had never wanted to kill anyone else in my life. But if I had the chance, I wouldn't think twice about taking Brian K.

Morris' life. Maybe I was never going to stop carrying such hatred around. Ms. Kim would say healing would never take place with such a dark mindset, but rage had become my best friend.

No medicine from a doctor was going to cure me.

"Off topic, Dad, but I've been learning a lot about the landfill next door to your building."

Dad folded his napkin carefully before sliding it away from him. "The stench was especially horrible today."

"Just be careful."

"I'm always careful," Dad said with a smile.

"I know you are." I searched for the right words as to not sound like a lunatic. "There's so many things that can go wrong with it being so close to you. Just be prepared should any kind of catastrophe happen. Get out of there as fast as you can should something bad go down."

Dad looked puzzled. "Like what?"

I replied, "The weather forecast said strong storms were coming in tomorrow afternoon. Possibility of tornadoes. If one were to hit the landfill, it would be catastrophic. Make sure your phone's always charged and you know where all the emergency stuff is. Flashlight, first aid kit, radio."

"No worries," Dad said. "We keep the emergency supplies in the office. With the big tornado that hit in '11, we've become more prepared. I'm supposed to be the one who worries about you, Jonah."

There was no way to convey the kind of danger waiting for all of us. Not without sounding insane, anyway. I took a deep breath and decided to let it go. "Maybe I'm growing up or something."

"Don't worry about me, Son. The biggest threat to me is fighting the urge to vomit when the August heat makes the landfill smell even worse than it already does."

There was much more to fear than the landfill's stench. The world was filled with monsters of all kinds. Some had red, glowing eyes and wings, acting as an omen to an impending disaster. Or maybe it was our own government conducting gruesome experiments on kids. Others prey on small children playing in the park. These monsters destroy innocence and kill themselves before they can face the consequences of the atrocities they had committed. Monsters like Brian K. Morris.

And I was powerless against them.

CHAPTER 22

THE NEXT MORNING at school, Dylan was happy to report he had a good night's sleep. I did too. Unfortunately, Shannon and Brandon were just beginning their horrible journey into nightmare-hell. Throughout the day, students and teachers alike grumbled about their phone service going out repeatedly. My own phone kept losing service, and even the one Level 6 had given me was also dropping its signal.

Had the sky not looked so green, we would have gone to the landfill to join the other UFO hunters, but we rushed home instead. Dylan took Brandon in his truck, and I drove Shannon home since her car was having issues. It was hot and humid outside, and the ominous clouds churned above us when I drove down my street. Mom was already home, but Dad's car wasn't in the garage.

"Hurry inside," Mom yelled from the front porch.

The gust of wind threatened to knock my tiny mom off the steps. Branches from all the trees in our neighborhood were flying around everyone's front yard, and the TV in the living room blared the weather report. Mom struggled to shut the door behind us.

"Is Dad still at work?" I asked her.

"He's going to stay there," she replied. "They have a basement, so they'll be safe there. It's too dangerous to be out driving in this."

On TV, the meteorologist pointed to a huge splash of red and purple on the radar.

"We're under a tornado watch until eight o'clock," Mom said as she pulled a blue duffel bag from the cabinet in the laundry room. "Storm warning until four."

The tornado from 2011 was traumatic. We weren't too far removed from its devastation just a few years ago, and the familiar terror filled my body. It had been a Friday evening, and I wasn't feeling too good, so I decided to just go home and crash. The tornado had touched down in Corazon Park and destroyed anything in its path for twenty-two miles across our area. The twister completely leveled houses in our neighborhood. We were lucky. Other than some minor roof and siding damage, we had been spared. Dylan, Brandon, and Shannon's houses were also fortunate, but most of our neighbors weren't so lucky.

Adrenaline coursed through me, and all I could think about was the landfill. If the tornado were to hit it, it would scatter radioactive material all over the damn place, and Dad was at Ground Zero. The urge to grab my keys and go after him hit me right away, but I couldn't just leave Mom here by herself.

We always kept water and supplies in the basement. But the emergency duffel bag also held a first aid kit, flashlights, and a crank-operated radio with built in phone charger. I could tell from Mom's tension-filled face she too was terrified.

Mom left to get some things from the master bedroom. I checked my phone again, but it still wasn't working. Something hard continually smacked the side of our house, but when I checked, it was just one of the neighbor's trees slamming against their metal shed. The kitchen stove air vent started howling, and the lights and TV flickered before going out. Despite it being the middle of the day, it was as dark as night.

I flipped on my phone's light, and I went straight towards the master bedroom with the emergency duffel bag. Mom was clutching her purse when she nearly ran into me in the doorway.

"Let's head for the basement," she said.

Tornado sirens cut through the howling wind. I led Mom to the basement door, opening it and letting her go in first with my phone's light to help her see. Our basement was partially finished, but it was used mostly for storage. Mom dropped her purse on the old couch and went straight for the small windows. She immediately shut the heavy, wooden blinds.

"I'd try to call Dad, but my phone has no service," I said.

She squinted at my phone before sitting next to her purse on the couch to confirm. Mom took her own phone out of her purse and sighed. No signal. I sat down next to her, hugging the duffel bag as if it was a security blanket. The siren continued to wail, and the sound of debris slamming into the basement windows made us jump.

Mom whispered, "Our homeowner's insurance is going to skyrocket."

I studied her face to see if she was serious, and she actually cracked a smile. "Mom, that's the least of our worries."

With every ounce of my being waiting for the worst sound in the world, which was the freight train-roar of an actual tornado, I closed my eyes and sought my intuition to guide me. Was this the disaster the Mothman had been preparing us for? I did my very best to quiet my mind and not let my fear overwhelm me, but I couldn't concentrate enough to sense anything. Some prognosticator I turned out to be.

"Are you praying?" Mom asked me.

I didn't want her to worry. "Maybe."

"Nothing wrong with that," she said. "You must be

really scared to be praying right now."

We were never a religious family, but Mom tended to be the most spiritual out of all of us. My hands were sweaty from grabbing the duffel bag so hard. I opened my hands and let the bag fall to the carpeted floor.

I put my clammy hand on top of hers. "You have no idea."

When the tornado siren died away, Mom and I waited in the basement for a good thirty minutes before we ventured back upstairs. Still holding onto her purse, Mom looked outside the living room window. I went to the kitchen, and from there, I noticed a large tree limb had fallen next door.

"Doesn't look too bad," Mom said from the living room. "We'll have a little bit of a mess to clean up, and we'll have to inspect our exterior."

My phone vibrated in my pocket. A text message from an unknown caller had somehow gotten through.

Elijah Elijah Elijah Elijah Elijah Elijah Elijah Elijah

With a trembling finger, I deleted it. Another text chimed in, but this time, it was from Dad.

"All is OK here. Coming home soon."

"Dad said he's OK, and he's on the way home." I tried to let him know we were alright over here too, but

I had lost service again. "But I'm not able to reply."

"At least he's safe." Mom raised up her phone. "I don't understand it. Everyone I know has had issues all day. Doesn't matter what network they're on either."

The sky remained green, but there was still enough daylight breaking through to not need flashlights. After just thirty minutes, our lights came back on. Mom went to the TV and turned it on. According to reports, a small tornado had touched down in Maryville Heights nearby, but Bridgetowne had been spared. The twister had come within five miles of the landfill, however, before dissipating. That was a close call.

While I was relieved, I was even more fearful than before. The tornado. The downed cell phone service. These were mere precursors of what was to come. The Cardinals were playing the Reds tonight, which I assumed hadn't been cancelled. Baseball was important to just about every St. Louisan, but now, that importance took on a whole new meaning for me

I ran back downstairs to retrieve the emergency duffel bag. Something told me it would be needed upstairs soon.

After school the next day, the others and I met at my car. The Reds had beaten the Cardinals 6-3 the

previous night, so the end of the world hadn't come. Dylan looked more like himself, and he was absolutely his energetic self that afternoon. Shannon and Brandon, however, still looked weary from the previous night's horrible dreams of death and destruction, although neither dreamed about a tornado this time. That bad omen had come and gone.

Everyone's cell phones still had choppy service, however.

"We have to go to the landfill," Brandon said. "I heard there's literally over a hundred people there right now."

Shannon rubbed her eyes. "If we go, we stay just for an hour. No longer. I'm exhausted."

Dylan said, "I don't mind seeing the Mothman. As long as it's from a distance, I'm good."

After throwing our backpacks into my trunk, we got into my car and headed for the landfill. The Cardinals and Reds were going to play again, but later that night at seven-fifteen. We had a good four hours before we would have to hold our breaths while watching the game on TV.

Brandon was right. There had to be at least a hundred people in front of the landfill's front gate. This time, four news vans were parked along the street. News crews interviewed hand-picked individuals from the crazy crowd. The police were there too, keeping the mass of people at a distance from the facility. The whole area buzzed with UFO hunters, eager to capture more footage of the triangular crafts visiting the area at all times of the day now.

"The Mothman needs to show up," Dylan said. "If it does, everybody here will go totally ape-shit, and the news crews will catch it on video too."

We kept our distance from the bulk of the crowd, instead finding a spot to sit on the street's curb. If the Mothman were to make an appearance, it would create such a crazy spectacle. Maybe if others saw it, the weight on our shoulders would be alleviated. After an hour of waiting, however, I had a feeling all of these people were going to be disappointed today. Shannon fought her sleepiness the whole time, and she whined about going back home.

When we stood up, I couldn't shake the feeling we were being watched. I spun around toward the western side of the industrial street, and the familiar black Mercedes rolled into view. It parked in another side parking lot, but neither agent stepped out.

This time, Agent Perkins was behind the wheel. He removed his fedora and kept his eyes trained on me. I pulled out my Level 6-issued phone and waved it around. They still didn't make a move. Instead, they sat there staring at us.

"It's time to go," I said.

Shannon stopped all of us from heading back towards my car. "My phone! I'm getting an actual call!"

At that exact moment, all four of us had our phones either vibrate or ring. My screen said it was from another unknown caller, and my instinct was to decline the call. Reluctantly, we each answered our phones.

"Many will die."

It was Elijah's voice, I was sure of it. Brandon looked like he was about to drop his phone, and Dylan fought back tears as he kept his cell pressed against his ears. Shannon was the first to turn hers off and ask the others, "Who just called you?"

I replied, "It was Elijah. He said many will die."

Dylan's wide eyes blinked rapidly at me for a moment before he said, "It was my grandpa, and he said the exact same thing."

"My aunt called me," Brandon said. "Many will die."

We all turned to Shannon as she wiped a stray tear from her face. "Mine was from my dad."

Shannon had lost her father a while ago, long before she had moved to St. Louis. He had been in a car accident coming home from work when she was just a baby.

"How is this even possible?" Dylan asked the group.

There was no answering his question. Without saying a word, we walked back to my car, glancing over our shoulders at the Level 6 agents every few seconds. They still hadn't budged. Maybe they were here to harass the other people who had gathered here to spot the UFOs.

Just before I could turn the ignition, my Level 6 phone vibrated. I pulled it out of my pocket and stared at it for a long time before answering the call.

CHAPTER 23

I JUMPED BEHIND the wheel and shut the door, and the others got inside my car and huddled around me. "Hello?" I switched the phone to speaker, but all got from my Level 6 phone was thick static. "Hello?" I asked louder.

A faraway voice sliced through the interference. "Hello, Jonah Ashe."

It was definitely not Dr. Park. "Who is this?"

"My name is Karl Ardo." Static blared from the phone's speakers, but it dissipated when the voice continued with, "I am not with Level 6."

Shannon, Dylan, and Brandon's eyes just about bulged out of their sockets. A lump formed in my throat, and I tried to pick just one question to throw at Karl. "If you're not with Level 6, who are you with?"

"I'm with no one, Jonah Ashe."

Shannon couldn't hold it in any longer. "How the hell did you get this number?"

"It doesn't matter, Shannon Crash."

Dylan's face was so ghost white, he looked like he might pass out. He whispered, "How did he know her name?"

"The same way I know your name, Dylan Mitchell. I also know Brandon Collier sitting next to you."

Every nerve ending in my body shivered with cold electricity. I had a million questions for Karl Ardo, but my throat failed to produce a sound. The harsh static returned, filling the car with its awful crackling.

"Put your phone down, Brandon." Karl Ardo said. "There's no point in researching my name. You'll find absolutely nothing."

Brandon looked as if someone had stabbed him between the shoulder blades. He turned off his phone and pushed it into his pocket.

I slowly scanned the area through the windshield and side window. Karl Ardo had to be out there watching us. Was this Agent Stewart or Agent Perkins messing with me? No one was near us, and I didn't see anyone watching us either. The crowd remained near the landfill's gates, waiting to catch the next UFO sighting.

"Jonah, I'm not anywhere near you. There's no need to look around for me."

Dylan actually let out a high-pitched squeal through his tight lips. "This is so messed up."

Shannon bent over the phone in my hand. "Are you

some kind of mind reader?"

"Oh no, I'm not a mind reader," Karl Ardo replied.

"Prove it." Shannon opened her backpack and shoved her hand inside the small pocket. Something jingled inside, and she kept her balled fist inside the compartment. "What do I have in my hand right now, Karl?"

Static swept over his voice, but it parted long enough for Karl Ardo to say, "Two quarters, one nickel, and three pennies. It's the change you received from Beth O'Toole, the lunch lady with the red hair and round glasses. You purchased chicken nuggets, french fries, and a raspberry tea Snapple."

Even Shannon didn't know exactly what was in her grasp. She pulled her quivering hand from her backpack to reveal its contents. We all could see clearly that she did, in fact, have two quarters, one nickel, three pennies. Since I had lunch with her, Karl Ardo was accurate about what Shannon had bought for lunch, and the lunch lady looked just as he had described.

"What do you want?" I asked.

"I want to help you. All four of you have been plagued with such terrible visions, especially you, Mr. Ashe. Level 6 is to not be trusted. To say they have grossly misunderstood what is happening is an understatement. They have no idea what the truth is."

I was afraid to ask, but I did anyway. "What is the

truth?"

"You have been misled. Tricked by a great evil. It has penetrated your minds. Your nightmares and visions come from this sinister force to drive you mad. To make you desperate. It aims to interfere with your lives. Disrupt it. Your world has been turned upside down ever since…"

The static swept in again.

I said, "Ever since we first saw the Mothman."

"Exactly. What you call The Mothman is actually an evil entity. It has existed for thousands of years, corrupting the thoughts of mankind. It makes you see things that are simply not there. It wants you to second guess yourselves. It delights in seeing you miserable. Reject its deception."

Dylan said, "It sounds a lot like the Devil."

"It does, doesn't it?" Karl paused again, letting the wave of static wash over our connection before continuing. "Throw this phone away. Refuse to talk to Level 6. Never speak of the Mothman ever again, and you take away its power. Only then can you regain your lives."

I had the urge to throw the phone out of the window, but I couldn't even move. "What about you? Are you even human?"

"I am whatever you want me to be. Human, dog, bird. Truth. I am the truth, Jonah Ashe. I know the pain you carry inside. You relive the day your brother died over and over again. I can feel your anguish. Your anger. Your guilt."

My hand trembled, nearly dropping the phone. Shannon was quick enough to reach out and steady my arm. There was no way for my brain to process what was actually happening. I couldn't comprehend who or what Karl Ardo was. I had suspected Karl Ardo existed outside our plane of reality.

I dug deeply through my fear to find my own truth. I needed my intuition to speak to me now. My inner voice, which was the real me from within, would speak to me through this nightmare. Was Karl Ardo the truth? Or was it the Devil himself?

I asked him, "How do you know so much about me? About all I've been through?"

"Jonah, the evil has infected your mind. It seeks to control you through fear. It makes you question your very identity. You and I both know who you are. You are Jonah Ashe, a good young man who wants to protect those he loves."

Shannon leaned over to say something, but more static overtook the call. Startled, I dropped it onto the floor. A high-pitched screech replaced the static, and it was so loud, we had to cover our ears. In a flash, the sound disappeared. The phone went blank. Shannon had her hand on her chest, trying to control her breathing. Dylan and Brandon were pressed hard against the back seat. They had drawn their legs up, as if they were terrified of a giant rat crawling on the floor mats.

"You need to literally throw that phone out the door," Brandon said. "You heard Karl Ardo. Level 6 is evil. Maverick already warned you about them. The Mothman has infected our minds. I want to sleep again."

Dylan tried to comfort Brandon by patting him on the shoulder. "What should we do?"

"I don't trust this Karl Ardo guy," Shannon said. "I don't trust Level 6 either. This whole thing has gone up another three notches in the creep-o-meter, that's for sure."

I bent down and picked up the phone. I pressed the home button, but it was dead. Battery was completely drained.

"What is it?" Shannon closed in on me with concern in her eyes. "Tell us what you're thinking."

All I had was my gut feeling, so that's what I decided to go with. "Karl Ardo is so not the truth. Karl Ardo is actually the evil entity it spoke of. It doesn't want us to be prepared for what's coming. It wants to shut us up. I'm not going to partner-up with Level 6 either. The only ones I can trust are you guys."

"I can go along with that," Dylan said.

Shannon nodded. "Me too."

Brandon wiped his forehead. "OK. Trusting you guys is no problem. But still, you think Karl Ardo is maybe an alien or something?"

I had absolutely nothing to base my feelings on, but my intuition was speaking to me loud and clear. "If the Mothman is the yin, then Karl Ardo is the yang. They are two sides of the same coin. They're not aliens in the traditional sense, but they come from a different dimension, maybe. And every once in a while, they're able to travel to our plane of existence."

"Why would they do that?" Shannon asked me.

"I'm not sure. I think they're fighting," I replied.

"Fighting for what?" Dylan asked.

I started the engine and put the car in drive. "Fighting over us. They're battling over who we should believe. Maybe they're fighting for our very souls."

Even listening to the radio wasn't going to let me escape all the weirdness. Just about every station in St. Louis was reporting on the strange sightings of UFOs now being seen all over the city, not just at the landfill. People panicked. Gun sales were way up, and grocery stores were running out of non-perishable food and bottled water.

After dropping Shannon off at her house, my inner voice spoke to me again. I wasn't in the mood, and I tried to ignore it, but the urgency tugged at me until I acknowledged it. Well Springs. That's where my intuition was telling me to go. I thought about calling Shannon to see if maybe I could turn back around and have her come with me, but I decided not to. This was something I had to do on my own.

I called Mom to tell her I was studying at Dylan's house. Traffic getting to the western side of the Missouri River was awful. How could anyone tolerate this commute every day? Using my phone's GPS, I eventually got to Well Springs an hour later. The parking lot was actually pretty busy, and lots of walkers filled the hiking trail. Piles of fallen tree limbs were scattered all over the place from the previous day's storms.

Paranoia struck me like a stray baseball smacking the back of my head. The black car entering the park didn't resemble an antique Mercedes Benz, but I still sprinted to the narrow path leading to the gravel stairway. I must have looked ridiculous, but I stretched out my calves before beginning the climb up the seventy-five-foot mound encapsulating the radioactive containment.

I kept a steady pace all the way to the top. My legs and lungs burned as I staggered towards the benches. I found myself all alone way up there, so I plopped down on the wooden bench and stared up at the sky. I must have laid there for at least twenty minutes when I heard approaching voices coming up the man-made mountain.

A young couple in their twenties made their way up to the viewing platform. The guy remained leaning on the railing while his girlfriend went to one of the plaques. They both glanced over at me before ignoring me for the next five minutes. When they decided they had had enough, they left me alone again.

I went back to sky-gazing. The sun wouldn't set for another two hours, and the Cardinals would be playing the second game in their series against the Reds maybe half an hour after that. It didn't matter. It felt good to just lie there by myself, staring up at the thin clouds.

The sound of rushing water came to my ears. Or was it static? The sound disappeared; it was just paranoia. I had just started to think about everything Karl Ardo had said when a man's voice shook me from my daydreaming.

"This is where we first met," Agent Stewart said as he approached.

I hadn't heard them coming up at all, which wasn't surprising.

Agent Perkins tipped his hat. "See anything interesting up here?"

"Nope." I went back to staring at the sky. "Not a damn thing. Why are you here? Not enough excitement at the landfill?"

"We're not big fans of crowds," Agent Stewart replied. "Besides, we had a feeling you had something new to tell us."

I decided to play a little mind game of my own. "What if I do?"

"You're supposed to call Dr. Park," Agent Perkins said.

I pulled their phone from my left pocket and held it up. "Battery's dead."

Agent Stewart took it from my hands and handed it to his partner. After inspecting it with both hands, he handed it back to me. The screen was lit up, and it had a fully charged battery.

"How the hell did you do that?" I asked them.

Agent Stewart ignored my question. "What's happened since meeting with Dr. Park?"

I sat up. "Wait. Why don't I hear static in my head anymore?"

Agent Perkins smiled. "Because we decided to be nice. As long as you answer our questions truthfully, we won't push you."

"Push? Is that what you call it?" I put their phone back in my pocket. "If it keeps you jokers out of my head, I'll talk."

Even though they weren't trying to bend my will again, I felt a strange pulsing against my middle ear. It felt as if I was in an airplane and my ears needed to pop. I ignored whatever they were doing by embracing my determination. I decided, out of my own freewill, to just lay it all out on the table for these two asshats.

I told them, "I'm going to assume you know who Karl Ardo is."

The agents exchanged nervous glances.

"I'll take that as an affirmative." I stood up to face them. "He told me you're not to be trusted. You're working against humanity. He doesn't want me talking to you or anybody about what's happening here in town."

Agent Perkins asked me, "Did you meet Karl Ardo?"

"No. He called me," I replied. "On your phone."

"Our phone?" Agent Stewart snapped his fingers at me, so I gave it back to him. He swiped through a couple screens. "There's no record of any incoming calls."

He handed the phone back to me. I glanced at it quickly before putting it away. "Something tells me Karl Ardo doesn't leave much of any kind of trace. Who, or what, the hell is he? Is he a ghost or something?"

Agent Stewart gave me the closest thing he had to a smile. "You already know the answer, Jonah."

"Yeah, but multidimensional being just sounds so much better coming from secret government agents," I said. "You've been chasing him for a long time too, huh? Probably as long as you've been hunting the Mothman."

Agent Perkins nodded. "Karl Ardo is not to be

trusted."

"I learned about irony in eighth grade language arts," I said. "You won't need to use your mind abilities to know I don't trust any of you. Here's my assessment: Level 6 doesn't give a rat's ass about anybody here. You're here to figure out all this stuff you don't understand. If there should be some kind of horrible disaster, Level 6 won't lift a finger to do anything to help anybody. You don't fully comprehend the Mothman or Karl Ardo, so you want to put them in cages and figure them out. Right?"

Once again, the two agents looked at each other nervously.

"Thanks for charging my phone with whatever super powers you guys have," I said. "If I run into the Mothman or Karl Ardo again, I will call Dr. Park. Scout's honor." Instead of giving them the three-fingered salute, I flashed them my middle finger. "Maybe you guys should check out East St. Louis. There's been reports of the Chupacabra running around over there."

Agent Stewart made a move towards me. He stood a good six inches taller than me. "We have the feather you gave Mrs. Lee. Don't worry, she won't blame you when she realizes it's missing."

The agents stood there for a minute or two before walking away.

For the third time, I sat down and put my head

down on the bench. Instead of looking up, I closed my eyes and focused on my breathing. I was tempted to take a peek to make sure the agents were truly gone, but I decided against it. Just as my body had fully relaxed, my own phone vibrated and jolted me from my peace. My screen indicated Luke Skywalker was calling me.

"Maverick?"

His voice broke through the static. "Hey, Cuz. What's up?"

The agents were indeed gone. "There's not enough time to even begin to explain," I answered. "But you just missed Level 6 by five minutes. Those two spooks were just here."

"Just be careful with those guys. If they wanted, they could shut you up. Forever." Again, the static overtook Maverick's voice at the end. "We're still up in Chicago. Looks like we'll be on our way back down to Cape Girardeau in a week."

My gut told me Maverick and Uncle Charlie weren't really going to be visiting St. Louis next week. "Sounds good," I told him.

The static died away a little bit. "The reason why I'm calling is because I just woke up from a three-hour nap, and I had a dream. You were in it. We were at an old-school drive-in movie theater, but there weren't any cars around. Two giant movie screens kept flashing stuff up. One screen kept showing dead bodies lying all around the place. The other one showed a baseball score."

My head started to pound. "Don't tell me. Cardinals 14, Reds 2."

"Yeah. That's exactly right." Maverick took a deep breath. "Aren't they playing tonight?"

"Game two of a three-game series here in town," I replied. "First pitch is at seven fifteen tonight."

Maverick said, "Whatever is going to happen, it's going to happen very soon."

My gut agreed with him. "I know."

"Just be careful, Cuz."

"Thanks Mav."

I was just about to hang up when I heard Maverick say one last thing: "Make sure to stay wherever you are for the next two hours, Jonah."

"What? Why?"

"In my dream, the Mothman comes to visit you," Maverick replied. "Are you somewhere up high. Like in a tower or balcony?"

I shouldn't have been so surprised by anything at that point. "Actually, I am. I'm on top of a seventy-five-foot mountain where a bunch of radioactive crap is buried underneath me."

Maverick said, "Damn. OK. Well, stay there. The Mothman is coming."

CHAPTER 24

I DOUBT I had even blinked for the two hours I waited at the top of the observation platform. Shannon, Dylan, and Brandon all texted me, saying they were watching the game. I lied and told them I was home watching it too. The park had become empty and eerily quiet. Even if Maverick hadn't warned me, I knew the Mothman was going to be there soon. In fact, Maverick said it would arrive at 7:27 exactly.

While staying seated on the bench, I kept my eyes upwards. Every airplane flashing its lights was the Mothman. The sky held just a sliver of daylight on its western edges when I saw a bright red light out in the distance. I confirmed with my phone that it was 7:27. After just a few short moments, it descended just below the clouds. I had to squint in order to make out its form. The Mothman's wings flapped with the grace of an eagle, yet it was definitely no bird. It circled high above me several times, like a vulture waiting for its victim to die. It finally flew behind the tall trees in the distance, and I lost sight of it.

Reluctantly, I left the safety of the bench. I stood in the center of the platform, waiting. Where had it gone? I did my best to stay calm, but my heart kept smashing against my chest. A heavy sounding whoosh from behind me caught my attention, and when I spun around, the Mothman stood a mere six feet away from me.

I immediately shielded my face from the blinding light. It ruffled its feathers before the intensity of its fireball eyes dimmed. This time, I was able to get a much better look at the creature standing in front of me. Its head was actually humanoid, but larger. And it had no nose. Instead, it had two small pinholes for nostrils. The Mothman's mouth was a short, horizontal slit. Its torso was likewise humanoid, but it was covered in gray scales. It had two long, muscular arms dangling at its sides. The massive feathers from its wings covered up the rest of its body, drawn together below the waist.

"I knew you'd be here," I said.

The creature emitted its strange vibrating grumble from its mouth. It seemed to glide across the ground, coming another couple of feet closer to me. My head filled with static, like an old radio trying to find a working channel. A hundred different voices echoed all around me until they formed one single voice.

Death is coming. I wasn't hearing him with my ears, but I swore the Mothman was transmitting its thoughts straight into my brain.

"I know. Does it have to do with the landfill?"

You must be prepared. He will need you when the moment comes.

"Who will need me? Dad? His office is right next to the landfill. Will he need my help?"

Be clear of mind. Let your illusions fall away.

Why did the Mothman have to communicate like a one-hundred-year-old Kung Fu Master? I was tired of all these riddles. "What illusions?"

The Mothman stood two feet taller than me, and it bent its back to come only inches from my face. Even though its red eyes weren't nearly as bright as before, I still couldn't look at them. The stink of burning metal made me gag.

Its form became hazy, as if it was turning into a ghost. Right before my eyes, it shape-shifted into the person I hated the most. Long, scraggly hair. Thick eyebrows. Black stubbles covered his long face. Brian K. Morris looked directly into my eyes just before he winked.

My body convulsed with raw hatred. What I saw made no sense, but it didn't matter. Without giving it a second thought, I unloaded my left fist into his face.

My knuckles cracked against his sharp cheek bone, the impact sending him reeling backwards. I grabbed onto his white shirt and pounded his face with my sore fist over and over again. Blood erupted from a cut above his right eye, then his nose exploded with snot and more blood. I busted his lip, smearing his teeth with crimson.

I shook his weakened body. "I will kill you!"

Brian K. Morris never flinched, but he became limp as I picked him up and threw him. He stumbled before his head smacked into one of the cement podiums. Blood smeared the memorial plaque on top of it. His lanky body collapsed and lay in a heap on top of the gravel.

"Rot in hell!" I picked up his head by his greasy hair and slammed his skull against the corner of the memorial, splattering the display with more of his rotten blood.

The child-killer didn't move.

My fist throbbed, and I wondered if I had broken something. But I didn't care. Boiling acid rumbled from my stomach until it erupted from my throat. I spewed everything I had for lunch onto the ground.

A hard, cold wind blew, chilling me to the core. Brian K. Morris' body turned to dust; a cloud of black ashes scattered and floated all around the observation platform. It became a whirling tornado of dark sand which grew taller until its swirling power knocked me backwards and to the ground. From within the black vortex, the Mothman stepped out and stood over my convulsing body.

Let go of your illusions. The time is at hand.

I was drained. I had no fight left in me. No anger left to burn. I just wanted to know one thing now. "Is my brother in heaven? The afterlife?" I felt stupid for asking such a question, but I was beyond embarrassment. "Is Elijah in the other dimension?"

The Mothman backed away. Its wings shook, as if it was ready to take flight. Either I was having a full-on seizure, or the ground was shaking. The Mothman leaped high into the air. With one flap of its majestic wings, it shot straight up into the sky. It streaked behind the trees before launching straight up into the clouds.

How was I going to explain how I had broken my hand? I inspected it using my camera flashlight, and any trace of blood or injury was gone. I opened and closed it, wiggling my perfect fingers. I stood up and went to where I had thrown up, but my barf was still there.

Before I could even process what had just happened, my phone came to life. It was Shannon.

"Cards up 4-0 in 2nd inning."

The end of the world was coming tonight.

When I got home, both Mom and Dad were in the living room watching the game on TV. I could only recall a handful of times when they'd watch the game together. Usually, it was Dad who had it on while doing some work, only half-paying attention. Mom wasn't much of a baseball fan, but she found small talk about the Cardinals was a good way to break the ice with new clients.

"If you're hungry, I wrapped up a plate of brisket in the fridge," Mom said from the couch.

My stomach protested with a gurgle. I sat across from them. "How are we doing?"

"We're now up six-to-nothing, top of the third inning," Dad replied. "Did you and Dylan get a lot of work done?"

"Yeah." I thought about grabbing the food, but my stomach was too tied in knots to digest it. "Have either of you heard about some really strange things going on around town?"

It took Mom a moment to answer, "Actually, yes. I've had more cancellations in one week than I've had all year. We've also had a lot of other realtors out sick."

I turned to Dad. "How about you?"

"Other than the crowds blocking the street by

work?" He glanced at Mom. "You know, now that you mention it, we've had a lot of employees out sick this week too. And a few more requested time off for tomorrow. There has to be some kind of flu pandemic going around."

All of this made perfect sense. "You know why all those people are outside your building, right?"

Dad replied, "No protest, but someone at work said they're UFO chasers or something."

"That's right," I said. "There's been reports of UFOs above the landfill. One day, the others and I saw it for ourselves. Sure enough, a triangular UFO flew just below the clouds right over us."

Mom looked as if she might jump up and call the psych ward to cart me off right there and then. Dad was speechless.

"We don't know what they are," Dad finally said. "That's why they're unidentified. You think they might be classified military aircraft?"

"I have no idea," I answered. "But this stuff is all over the news."

"You know how much I hate the news," Mom said. "I don't pay attention to any of it these days."

I couldn't blame her there. "There's some crazy stuff going on all around us right now. That's why all of your employees are missing all of these days at work. They're all struggling with the feeling something terrible is about to happen. They can't sleep at night. Horrible nightmares make them miserable. Have either of you had similar problems?"

Mom's worried face softened a bit. "Yes. I haven't had much sleep the last several days. I had a bad nightmare just last week. Or was it just last night? I dreamed about people dying. I think there was a bomb or something."

"You didn't tell me about that," Dad said to her.

Mom said, "They're just bad dreams. Are you having any nightmares too, Bill?"

Dad looked like he didn't want to answer her. His eyes darted from left to right, as if he was trying to come up with a good lie to tell us. "I've been stressed at work the last two weeks, so I haven't been sleeping well either."

I leaned forward. "Are you having nightmares like the rest of us, Dad?"

"I have to admit, yes."

"What were they about?" Mom asked him.

Dad put his head down. "Similar to yours, I guess. People were dead all around me. Not from a bomb. In my dream, it was from a giant tsunami."

There was something more Dad was hiding from us.

"What else, Dad? Was there someone in particular in your nightmare?"

He got up from the couch and started to pace. "I don't want anyone to get too upset with me, but yes,

Jonah. Your brother showed up in a couple of my dreams. I've been thinking a lot about him since your birthday."

Mom pulled him back to the couch and wrapped her arms around him. "You need to tell me these things."

I went over to Dad and put my hand on his shoulder. "When we had dinner the other night, all of this was on your mind?"

"It was," he replied.

"This has been hard on all of us," I said. "And talking with you at dinner, it made me realize I've been selfish. I never really stopped to think about how Elijah's death has affected you two. I'm sorry. We're not the only ones plagued with these nightmares and visions either. Something big is going to happen. Something terrible."

Mom and Dad went back to looking at me like I was crazy.

"Can you stay home from work tomorrow?" I asked them.

"I planned on working from home anyway," Mom said.

Dad shook his head. "I can't. We've got an acquisition finalizing next week, and I need to get a lot of work done by then."

"Don't you feel it, Dad?" I got down on one knee. "Your gut feeling telling you we're on the verge of a terrible catastrophe? We all feel it. The whole city feels it. Most are blaming it on stress and other stuff. People are buying guns, food, and water, and they're starting to make peace with unfinished business as if the end of the world was coming."

"End of the world?" Dad's rational mind was on full power. "Come on, Jonah."

"Maybe not literally," I said. "Mom, can you admit to having that gut feeling?"

Mom reached out to touch the top of my head. "You know me, I have a fatalist streak in me."

"This goes way beyond a fatalist streak." I remained on my knee, begging them to admit what they were feeling deep inside.

"I'm not going to lie," she whispered. "I do feel like something terrible is going to happen. I thought maybe it was the bad storm from yesterday, but there's something else."

Dad rubbed his temples. "Work has worn me down, I admit. I'll take a week off after the acquisition is completed. OK? I haven't taken a day off in over a year, and it's time I took a break."

I pretended to be satisfied, and I went back to the other couch. "Sounds good, Dad."

Mom pointed to the big screen on the wall. "Looks like the Cards got another two runs."

I wondered if there had been some kind of faraway explosion, but the floor beneath our feet continued to rumble for too long. The picture frames in the main hallway rattled against the wall. Mom and Dad's glasses of wine shook on the coffee table but didn't topple over. I held onto the couch armrests while the constant rippling of the ground shook everything in our house. It lasted less than thirty seconds.

"That was a pretty good one," Dad said.

Mom remained clutching Dad's hand. "It was at least a 4.0."

All the ballplayers had stopped playing, and the announcers remarked about the earthquake that had shaken the stadium. The game resumed, and I watched for another five minutes before getting up.

"I'm exhausted." I walked towards the hall. "Goodnight."

"Hey Jonah," Dad called after me. "I promise. I'll take a week off. Maybe we can go on a fishing trip out at the Ozarks?"

We hadn't gone finishing in years. "That would be great."

My phone buzzed a couple of times, so I hurried to my bedroom. Shannon had texted every time the Cardinals scored a run, and Dylan and Brandon were hysterical along with her. After shutting my door and lying on my bed, I joined in the group panic-fest.

Before eleven o'clock, the St. Louis Cardinals had defeated the Cincinnati Reds 14-2.

Long after midnight, we waited for the sky to fall, but it never did.

"Nothing happened! Going 2 bed," Dylan texted.

Dylan and Brandon signed off, but Shannon called me.

"I talked to my parents," I told her.

She asked, "Did you tell them everything?"

"No way. I was vague enough. They both have been having similar nightmares, though. They also said something about a bunch of their co-workers missing a lot of work this week."

"My mom mentioned something similar," Shannon said. "I don't like sitting around waiting for Armageddon."

I knew exactly what she was talking about. "Me neither. I hate feeling helpless."

"I kept thinking about Karl Ardo all evening. Do you really think he is the bad guy?" Shannon asked.

"I do. I'm sure of it," I replied.

Shannon took a deep breath. "Would that make the Mothman the good guy?"

"Yeah, I guess it would. I know it seems all messed up that a winged demon creature isn't the villain in our story." I debated whether or not to tell her about my Mothman encounter at Well Springs earlier. My brain was too exhausted to go into it. "My initial gut feeling stands."

"I hope we all don't die tomorrow, Jonah."

There was no way I was getting any sleep that night. "Me too."

CHAPTER 25

THE NEXT MORNING in the school parking lot, all four of us were complete wrecks. No one had gotten any sleep the night before. We decided to meet after school and figure out what to do next. Brandon especially looked disheveled with his hair sticking up. The dark circles around Dylan's eyes had returned. Shannon was dragging ass. If some kind of emergency was going to happen today, none of us were going to be much help to anyone.

At lunch, Shannon and I picked at our food and didn't talk much. We were lost in our thoughts, trying to figure out our place in all of this. For me, all I could think about was how I had killed a make-believe Brian K. Morris the previous evening. I didn't think I had the capacity to be so violent, so full of hatred and evil. It disgusted me. At the same time, I felt like a thousand-pound weight had been lifted from my chest. It was as if all the fuel that kept my fire of rage burning had been exhausted.

"I know one thing," Shannon finally said. "I'm supposed to be with you when the shit hits the fan."

I let out a nervous laugh. "Am I the one who needs your rescuing?"

"All my nightmares point to that, yeah." Shannon shut her lunch bag having only taken a few bites of her sandwich. "You're not leaving my sight for the rest of the day."

"Your sleep deprivation is talking," I said with a chuckle. "You plan on following me around until school's over."

I got up to throw away my water bottle. "I am one-hundred percent sure my dad will need my help when the time comes."

Shannon tossed away her practically uneaten lunch. "Then I'll be the one to help you help your dad."

I said, "Maybe we should skip out the rest of the day."

"I would, but I have a test fifth hour," Shannon said. "After school, I'm going to be your shadow."

I led her to the hallway towards our lockers. "That's a relief, because I have to go to the restroom."

The mirrors in the boys' restroom were never completely clean, and I thought maybe the smeared dirt played a trick on me. When I reached up to touch my right ear, my reflection was just a fraction of a second behind me. Hysteria was getting the better of me. I raised both of my hands and wiggled my fingers, and my reflection stood still. My own voice echoed in the bathroom.

Elijah. Elijah. Elijah. Elijah.

"Is that you, Elijah?" I asked my reflection.

The image in the mirror remained still.

Wake from your slumber.

Something in the corner of my mind continued to pick at me. "I wish I understood."

You've let go of your anger. Now, the time is at hand.

I touched the mirror, but my reflection still refused to move. "What are you trying to tell me? Talk to me, Elijah."

When I moved to turn on the cold water, my reflection moved as I did. All was right with the world again. I splashed some cold water on my face, half expecting my reflection to disappear altogether. Even if it was synced perfectly to my movements again, I still felt disconnected from my own image.

I was about to leave the restroom when the ground shuddered beneath me.

The hallway filled with panic. Students and teachers alike staggered to get underneath reinforced doorways, and something crashed and shattered in the lobby. I stumbled into the lockers, along with a few others, and we held on until the tremor stopped.

Several of the teachers started to corral everyone back into the cafeteria to take cover under the tables. I found an open spot away from the large windows, and we all waited underneath the long tables. A couple of students started to cry, but a few of them were laughing.

When we got the all clear signal from the school bell buzzing three times in a row, the teachers directed the students out the doors. We followed them outside, putting some distance between us and the school building. I found Shannon right away, and she looked like she was on the verge of an anxiety attack. Dylan and Brandon had fourth hour together, and they stayed with their class long enough for their teacher to include them with his head count before they met us in the parking lot.

"That was a big one," Dylan said.

The four of us sat on the curb. Many of the other students plopped down on the grass, texting their parents they were OK. We overheard a couple of teachers talking, saying there was very little damage, just some stuff falling off shelves but nothing major. Each teacher sent a designated student to run towards makeshift stations to submit the roll call and list of any missing students.

Administrators talked on their radios, checking in with all the teachers and making sure everyone was accounted for. Amazingly, it had been an orderly evacuation without any hint of panic. The four of us, however, knew this was just the beginning.

"You think they're going to make us go back into the building?" Shannon asked the group.

"Maybe," I replied. "But we're already past the halfway point in school. They might just dismiss us. I'm pretty sure parents will be picking up their kids early."

In the distance, the sound of firetrucks and sirens caught our ears. Surveying the area all around the school, I didn't see evidence of any damage. Windows all looked intact, and nothing looked broken.

We sat for over an hour before the teachers finally dismissed us for the day.

"What should we do?" Brandon asked me.

Dylan pulled out his car keys. "I have a feeling I should be at home."

Brandon chimed in, "Me too."

"Let's all go home and make sure everything is OK," I suggested. "Then maybe we should meet somewhere afterwards."

"Works for me," Dylan said. He motioned for Brandon to go with him. "Be careful, guys."

Shannon followed me to my car. "You know you're not leaving my sight, right?"

"I should drop you off at your house first to check on everything," I said.

"My mom is still at work. She said she's OK." Shannon crossed her arms. "You're not the only one with a gut feeling, you know."

I unlocked my car doors with my key fob. "What does your gut feeling tell you right now?"

Shannon jumped into my car first. "I don't think we're going to be meeting with Dylan and Brandon later today."

I had that same feeling too.

Mom was glued to the television when Shannon and I got to my house. "They said it was a 4.5 magnitude, and the epicenter was a town called Barlow in Western Kentucky."

"That's the New Madrid fault," Shannon said. "Again."

"I wish your dad would just come home," Mom said. She picked up her phone as if she was going to call him, but she put it back down on the coffee table. "I got through to him just fine the first time, but my service has been down since then."

Shannon glanced at her own phone. "I talked to my

mom for a bit too, but I don't have service anymore either."

"Is she OK?" Mom asked her.

"She's good, Mrs. Ashe."

I started to feel lightheaded. "We're just going to sit outside for a little bit, Mom. We'll be in the backyard if you need us."

We walked out the sliding door and stepped out onto the back patio. It was a gorgeous day. Usually, it was hot and humid this time of year, but it felt absolutely perfect outside. We sat down at the table, but Shannon kept staring at me.

"What is it?" she asked me.

"I thought I was going to pass out in the living room," I answered. "I feel better now."

Shannon didn't seem convinced. "What's going on with you?"

"Last night, I went to Wells Park by myself."

Her eyes widened. "Are you crazy?"

"Maybe." I checked my phone, and I still had no service. "Maverick called me and said he had a dream about the Cardinals beating with Reds 14-2 too. Then he said the Mothman was for sure going to come to me again."

"Did it?"

"Yeah, it did," I replied. "It spoke to me again."

Shannon put both hands on her mouth in horror.

"It telepathically told me I need to stop hanging

onto my hatred and let go of my illusions." I decided to not bring up how the Mothman shape-shifted into Brian K. Morris and that I had killed him. That was too many levels above weird for me to share, even with Shannon. "The time was at hand."

"Hanging onto hatred and letting go of illusions?" Shannon shook her head. "Is the Mothman a psychologist or something?"

"I asked about my brother. I asked if Elijah was in heaven."

"What did it say?" Shannon asked.

I exhaled a shaky breath. "It said no, not yet. What does that mean?"

"And what illusions do you need to let go of?" Shannon asked.

"It has something to do with my brother." I didn't have the energy to push away the truth anymore. I had no desire to fight the inevitable. "I'm in denial."

Shannon's eyebrows crinkled. "In denial about what?"

I was about to think my answer out loud when my phone buzzed, even though it still showed no service. "Hello?"

The static was so loud, I had to hold it away from my face. Eventually, the interference died away.

"Go now. You must go."

"Elijah?" I put the phone on speaker so Shannon could hear. "Elijah, is that you?"

No.

But his voice. It was my own.

"Jonah?" It felt weird saying my own name, but at that moment, it no longer belonged to me. "Is that you?"

Yes.

Shannon slapped my shoulder. "What the hell?"

Go now. You must go.

The static seemed to explode from my phone's tiny speakers until it completely died. I pulled the car keys from my pocket and headed for the driveway. Shannon struggled to catch up with me.

"Are you going to explain all of this?" she asked me.

I unlocked the doors. "Yes. If we survive."

"I don't like that answer." Shannon held her door open. "Where are we going?"

I got behind the wheel. "To go save my dad's life."

CHAPTER 26

EVERYONE ALWAYS SAID I drove like an old man, but for the first time in my life, I exceeded the speed limit by thirty miles per hour as I sped down Rock Road while Shannon kept trying to call Dad on my phone. Her service was out too, and even the car radio broadcasted a low hum no matter the station. My intuition was replaced by a panicked desperation. I knew it was much more than my imagination flashing images of buildings collapsing and dead bodies on the ground. All the destruction I saw in my mind was to be our immediate future.

"Jonah." Shannon tapped my shoulder. "You need to pull over."

I glanced into my rearview mirror. The flashing red and blue lights made me instantly sweat. I had never been pulled over before, but I knew I couldn't stop for any reason.

I pressed down harder on the gas pedal. "I can't."

"Are you serious?" Shannon looked like she might reach over and grab the wheel. "You can't outrun the cops."

My head filled with static. Both of my hands went numb. I thought I might pass out while hurling my Toyota down a main road at seventy miles per hour. At first, I assumed I had hit a pot hole. It felt as if I had run over a speed bump. The pavement shook violently beneath my tires, and it took all of my strength to keep the wheel steady. The very earth underneath convulsed with violent fury. Shannon screamed when a gas station sign tumbled and smashed just several yards in front of us. I swerved to avoid hitting it and nearly clipped a red truck in the other lane.

Cars veered off the road, smashing into curbs and each other. Several more store signs shattered when they fell from high above and slammed into the street. Powerlines snapped, raining fiery sparks in every direction. We were less than a mile from Dad when my car hit the buckled pavement. With a harsh jolt as we smacked against the concrete, we went airborne, crashing back onto the road with so much force, I tasted blood on my tongue.

The rattling intensified, and it felt as if the ground was moving like a stormy ocean. Seismic waves hurled us back into the air. We belly-flopped off the road, into the grass, but the rear wheel caught the curb with an explosion of metal on concrete. My head throbbed from the impact, and I wondered if I had suffered a concussion. It took all of my effort not to throw up.

I turned the car back onto the road, but I felt the rear dragging behind us. There wasn't time to inspect the damage. I stopped the car, put it in park, and threw open my door. We weren't too far from Dad's building, and we had no choice but to go the rest of the way on foot. Without saying a word, Shannon followed me across the road.

We stumbled onto the industrial road, fighting hard to keep our balance. Another shock sent me into the air. When I hit the ground, it felt as if a sword had been thrust right through my chest. I struggled to fill my lungs with air, and I thought I just might die.

Shannon crouched down and held my hand. "You're OK. Just got the wind knocked out of you."

The earth continued to tremble underneath us. In all the disaster movies, earthquakes seemed to simply shake violently and create huge cracks in the ground. But this was entirely different. It was as if the ground had become a tumultuous tsunami, with one wave followed by another one.

I couldn't comprehend the violence of the earthquake ratcheting up even higher, but that's exactly what it did. The rows of pine trees to our left danced wildly, and the sounds of explosions and crashes echoed from the main road. All we could do was watch the destruction unfold all around us. A large, white industrial building just a few blocks away caved in, and blood-curdling screams of terror echoed from the leveled structure.

Shannon kept her arms around me, and we braced ourselves for what seemed like hours until the strength of the tremors subsided.

"Let's go!" I got to my feet and pulled Shannon up. "We're just a couple of blocks away."

We hurdled over broken glass, chunks of concrete, and huge slabs of aluminum siding as we raced down the street. Bloodied and disoriented people littered the area, crying and yelling for help that was not going to be coming. The deli around the corner from Dad's building was completely gone; the only proof of its prior existence was the broken sign lying on the ground. The road to Dad's work was completely blocked with a mountain of debris, so we cut through what had been an alley between two buildings.

Amazingly, the alley wasn't blanketed with too many obstacles. A group of machinists in their dust-covered uniforms emerged from their partially collapsed building, but instead of heading towards the safety, they surrounded something down in the pavement. I didn't want to stop and look at what they were doing, but I couldn't help it. As we got closer, the five machinists got down on their bellies along the edge of what looked like a gateway to hell itself.

"A sinkhole," Shannon said as she stopped to catch her breath.

We watched the men pull someone up from the sinkhole, his face covered in blood. There must had been others down in there, as they continued to reach down into it.

Shannon pointed to the ground, which started shaking again. "We have to watch our step."

The quake started up again, which slowed us down even more. More bricks and concrete blocks rained down from the weakened industrial buildings. There was no way to watch out for sinkholes while simultaneously keeping an eye on the falling debris.

From afar, Dad's building looked relatively untouched. The massive warehouse doors had been ripped from their hinges, but other than that, the structure itself hadn't been damaged. Several evacuated employees made their way towards a clearing, but I didn't see Dad.

"It doesn't look too bad here," Shannon said from behind.

Adrenaline fueled my strength. The horrid stench of the landfill hit me so hard, I nearly gagged. Another small group of workers exited Dad's building through the front door, and none of them looked very injured. Maybe everything was going to be alright.

We sprinted around the congregation of employees, and before I could even come within ten feet of the front door handle, the ground beneath us seemed to explode under our feet. Shannon lost her balance and fell hard on her side. The door's glass shattered, and the next aftershock wave threw me backwards. I landed flat on my back onto the unforgiving sidewalk, once again knocking all the air from my lungs.

The building's swaying aluminum siding screeched as it twisted and contorted. It sounded as if a bomb had detonated inside, and the horrifying screams from within had me assuming the worst. After another few seconds, the swaying of the earth dissipated long enough for us to get back to our feet.

"I'm going in," I told Shannon. "You stay out here."

Shannon grabbed my arm. "I'm your shadow, remember?"

There was no time to argue. I carefully opened the front door, avoiding the large shards of glass protruding from the metal frame. The lobby was unrecognizable. All the chairs and tables lay scattered all over. I led Shannon towards the main corridor, which was filled with ceiling tiles and broken glass from all the fallen picture frames. Wounded employees retreated from their wrecked offices, looking right through us as they dashed towards the lobby.

Dad's office was towards the back of the building.

The main hallway had become so littered with crap, we had to climb our way through. The entire structure continued to shudder, as if it could collapse at any moment. My mind kept flashing more images of destruction, and I knew the building caving in on top of us wasn't our biggest threat.

We reached Dad's office, and I had to kick the door open since the frame had become disfigured. All five bookcases had toppled towards the center of the room, and just about every ceiling tile was now on the floor. Maybe Dad had evacuated early, and he was safe and sound outside.

"Dad?"

Amazingly, Shannon still had my phone. She redialed Dad's number, and it actually began to ring. From underneath all the rubble, the old school ringing of Dad's phone jolted me into action. The bookcases and cabinets were made out of metal, and I needed Shannon's help in pulling the first one away.

"Dad? Are you OK?"

His muffled voice broke through the mountain of debris. "Elijah? Is that you?"

With all the strength I had, I went to work on digging him out. The second cabinet was twice as heavy as the first one, and a huge piece of a metal beam lay on top of it. Shannon and I couldn't budge it.

I turned to Shannon. "Can you look for someone to help us?"

Without answering me, she bolted out the door.

"We're going to get some help, Dad. Just hold on."

I kicked away the heavy books and ruins. I could hear Dad struggling underneath, doing his best to climb out from the oppressive mound of debris, which gave me hope. My weakened body screamed at me to stop and take a breather, but I knew I had to keep going. I became light-headed, and the ringing in my ears made my head feel as if it just might explode.

Cold sweat soaked my shirt, and I used my sleeve to dry my forehead. I shut my eyes, and all I could see was the bright red flashing of the Mothman's eyes. Even after I opened my eyes, the pulsating orbs filled my entire field of vision. I pushed aside the sensation that I was going to faint.

Dad's voice somehow penetrated all the wreckage suffocating him. "Tell your mother I love her. I love you too, Son."

I summoned all of my strength and tried to slide the metal beam off the bookcase, but it was no use. "Don't talk like that. We're going to get you out of here, I swear."

"I did my best to help you."

I collapsed onto the huge pile of metal, concrete, and garbage. "You did help me. I know who I am now, Dad. I'm done pretending."

"We're here!" Shannon returned with two men at her side.

One guy was young and muscular looking. The other man was the polar opposite. He was elderly and scrawny, his thin, pale skin pulled taut against sharp bones. This geezer was going to be useless.

I fought back the urge to collapse with exhaustion. "Help me! He's underneath here."

The four of us grasped the metal bookcase. Amazingly, even the old man had some power behind his frail body. With our combined strength, we pulled it from the rubble. Dad thrust his hand through the pile. I took hold of it, and with help from the young guy, we yanked him out of the heap.

Dad gasped for air, but he wouldn't let go of my hand. "I thought I was going to die."

Fresh blood dripped from a long laceration across his forehead, and his white shirt was blackened with dirt. Other than some minor cuts on his arms, he looked to be OK.

I pulled him close, allowing him to lean on me as we left what remained of his office. "We have to get out of here now! We only have a few seconds!"

The other two guys didn't dare question my warning. Instead, they led us through the main hallway. Dad struggled to run, but we couldn't stop. Shannon brought up the rear, pausing to look behind her every once in a while. Another aftershock threatened to slow us down even more, but we battled to keep our balance and continue our evacuation. The entire building rattled again, swaying as if it was going to crumble and smash us within it.

We reached the lobby, and the ground's rumbling intensified. The old man actually took the lead. He and the other stranger shot through the now open doorway. With a piercing scream, Shannon pushed me and Dad out of the building. She tripped over the bent door frame, but she remained on her feet.

"Keep running!" I ordered everyone.

Wave after wave sent us all tumbling to the ground. The two guys helped us up, but I screamed at them to continue to put more distance between us and Dad's building. A dozen of his co-workers were sitting on the grass in a little courtyard, watching us as we approached.

"We need to get out of here!" I yelled at them.

A woman from marketing, whose name escaped me, said, "We're safe here."

I let go of Dad and grabbed her by the shoulder. "No one's safe here. We'll all die if we stay."

The earth shook with enough strength to throw us off balance and make anyone tumble awkwardly to the ground. Dad pulled me back to my feet and directed everyone further away from his building. We scurried towards a group of machinists sitting on the ground, and that's when the sensation of the entire planet being torn apart hurled us all onto the grass.

The deafening screams of twisting metal pierced

my eardrums, and had a volcano suddenly appeared in the middle of the industrial area and unleashed a mushroom cloud of fire and lava, I wouldn't have been surprised. Instead, Dad's building rumbled violently before disappearing with a mushroom cloud of smoke and soot. Dust and debris exploded in our faces, blinding us. Mother Earth was not just pissed, she was hungry, and she swallowed all fifty-thousand square feet of Dad's industrial stretch wrap company.

When the thundering and shaking stopped and the dust cloud finally thinned out, we gawked at the miniature Grand Canyon that had swallowed up not just Dad's building, but the other two next to it. The sinkhole had stopped less than ten feet from our group. The marketing lady crawled towards us, wiping the dirt from her face.

She whispered a weak thank you to me.

Dad sat up and put his arm around me. "You saved us." He wrapped his free arm around Shannon. "Both of you."

Shannon gave him a sideways smile. "Are you OK Mr. Ashe? Maybe you have a head injury." She pointed a thumb at me. "You called this guy Elijah."

"I'm sorry." Dad frowned. "I thought I was a goner, and I panicked."

"It's alright." I stared up at the bright blue sky, but there was no Mothman. "No more illusions."

CHAPTER 27

DAD WENT INTO boss-mode and met up with Mr. Ron O'Dell, his company's president, to make sure all of their employees were accounted for. I learned that the young man who had helped us was a sales guy. He just happened to be in town from Iowa. But we never saw the old guy ever again.

There was something familiar about the mysterious, elderly stranger. For several moments, I searched my memory banks. I called upon my hyperthymesia to recall if I had ever met him before. I didn't have to go back very far.

"What is it?" Shannon asked me as we walked slowly on the damaged street.

"The old man who helped us. I remember him from the very first night we saw the Mothman. He had driven by in an old blue pickup truck."

Shannon squinted her eyes in doubt. "Are you

sure?"

"We totally made eye contact that night," I replied. "Yes, I'm sure."

"Maybe that crazy-ass autobiographical memory of yours is playing tricks on you," she said with a laugh. "Or maybe you hit your head too hard."

I was going to argue, but then was not the time.

The wounded dragged their heavy feet all around us, aimlessly wandering all over the street. None of the industrial buildings on this block were more than two stories, luckily, but more than half of the buildings were either completely destroyed or on the verge of crumbling. Dad's building, along with two neighboring warehouses, were gone. Their remains lay inside the deep canyon, stacked on top of each other.

Just in case, everyone stood at least fifty yards away from the sinkhole. Helicopters hovered above the landfill. The screaming of sirens surrounded us in all directions. Every few minutes, the ground would rattle again, but these tremors were insignificant.

Shannon and I sat in the tall grass, in a large field filled with more wounded survivors. Neither of us spoke for a long time. We were both in shock, but for me, I was mostly dealing with the renewed clarity that came after escaping death. Illusions and denial had been like a comfy, warm blanket for so long, and now I felt vulnerable and naked. At least I knew who I was now.

"Well?" Shannon jabbed me with her sharp elbow. "Are you going to explain yourself?"

Instead of trying to formulate the right words, I just opened my mouth and spoke whatever came to my mind. "Losing my brother messed me up on many levels. The man who kidnapped and killed him could have just as easily taken me. It was a heavy burden to live with, especially for a nine-year-old. We didn't invent our own language, like some twins are known to do. But Mom liked to dress us alike, so we often switched names and pretended to be the other twin all the time, just to mess with everybody."

Shannon caressed my face with her hand.

"I not only had to deal with his death and how he died, but I choked on all that guilt. Our personalities were very different, but despite that, our bond went beyond the norm. In a way, we were two halves of one complete person. The guilt and the grief filling me up was a horrible combination."

"That makes sense," Shannon said.

"After he was killed, I took it further. Even before the funeral, I was already calling myself Jonah. From there, I continued to actually become him. I even changed my personality to match his. When Mom and Dad tried to correct me, I would throw tantrums and demand they acknowledge me as Jonah."

"I'm not going to lie," Shannon said. "That's really weird."

"I know." I checked my phone, even though I already knew it wasn't getting service. "Jonah's the one who actually has lighter eyes than me. He was the more outgoing brother, and like I said, I changed myself to become him. To live through him. Jonah was kidnapped, violated in the worst way, and killed."

A crease formed between Shannon's eyes. "So, you're actually Elijah."

I nodded. "My mom and dad played along, just for my sake. They tried to get me help, hoping I would eventually come out of it and face the truth. I was living a lie for so long, it became my truth."

"It's going to take some getting used to," Shannon said with a smile. "Calling you Elijah."

I wiped some of the dried blood from my chin. "Something tells me we've got other priorities to deal with first."

After a couple more hours, the police helped organize an evacuation of the area. The earthquake had caused soil liquefaction, creating a radioactive landslide that may or may not have contaminated the Missouri River. Without cell phone service, no one had any way of getting any kind of information on loved ones. After the Bridgetowne tornado, Dad had the idea of designating Corazon Park as our rendezvous place should we be separated during another disaster, but it was a good eight miles away.

Just from overhearing the police talking, it sounded like there were massive casualties from the 7.0 magnitude earthquake, which had originated along the New Madrid Fault. I prayed Mom had made it out of the house OK, and I hoped Brandon and Dylan, and their families, were likewise safe. It was stupid to keep checking my phone, but I did out of habit.

As the thousands of people walked down Rock Road, I kept glancing upwards. Shannon noticed this, and she too would look up for any sign of the Mothman. The only things in the skies were military helicopters surveying the damage or transporting troops to locations all around St. Louis.

The streets and highways had buckled and folded over, making them impassable. All of the bridges over the Missouri River were damaged, as were all the ones heading into Illinois. I had watched more than a dozen end-of-the-world movies, and nothing came close to the actual carnage and destruction we saw as we traveled down the road.

For the first few bloodied remains along the street, Dad warned us to look away. After a couple miles of more death, we had already become desensitized to the gore. Rubble and damaged buildings surrounded us on all sides, and not one structure had been spared. Firetrucks and other emergency vehicles were slowed down by all the obstacles on the roads, but all of them were heading to or from St. Paul Hospital. I couldn't imagine the horror all those doctors and nurses were having to deal with, and there were more wounded victims heading their way.

As we got closer to the park, it seemed thousands of others had had the same idea. Droves of survivors joined us along the main road leading to the lake. Several of the people around us talked about the park having been converted into a makeshift camp, which made perfect sense. There was a lot of open land that would be safe if there were to be any lingering aftershocks.

Dad hardly spoke during our slow journey towards Corazon Park. I knew all he was thinking about was Mom. I dug deep, hoping my intuition would give me some guidance. Even though I had an inkling she was OK, I had to admit to myself it was just wishful thinking.

Shannon also kept checking her phone. Her mom's work was pretty far away, closer to downtown. Trying to get out of the city would have been a true nightmare. All the ancient, towering buildings wouldn't have survived such an earthquake. Even if her mom was alright, it would be impossible for her to get to us out west.

"Are you OK?" Dad asked me as we finally started walking downhill.

"I'm fine," I replied. "It's all just a lot to process."

Dad turned to Shannon. "We will do all we can to get you back to your mother."

"Thanks, Mr. Ashe." Shannon looked behind us, staring at the long train of survivors. "I get the feeling nothing is ever going to be the same again."

I put my arm around her. "You're right. Everything has changed."

We reached Corazon Park just before dark. Soldiers surrounded the area, helping the wounded and setting up a base of operations for evacuees. Amazingly, even though we couldn't make or receive calls, Shannon finally received a text message from her mother. She had made it out of her building hours earlier, and she was stuck with her co-workers trying to find a way to get out of the city. Even though it would take at least until sometime tomorrow for them to reunite, Shannon cried with relief knowing her mom was alive and well.

People all around us started getting texts from their loved ones, and my phone buzzed along with them.

"It's from Mom!" I read her text twice just to make sure my mind wasn't playing tricks on me. I held up my phone to show Dad. "She's here already. Our whole neighborhood is at a camp near the Holloway Shelter. Just on the other side of the lake."

Dad had never been much of an athlete. He wasn't visibly out of shape, but he never exercised, except for cutting the grass or raking leaves. But he just about sprinted through the park, and he didn't slow down until after we had run about two miles around the lake. My lungs were on fire by the time Holloway Shelter came into view, and from the massive crowd of people surrounding it, it was going to take some time to pick out Mom from the masses.

A loud generator powered the mobile lights in the area, and soldiers were busy putting up small white tents everywhere. I thought about texting Mom back to help find her, but Dad called out and bolted towards the shelter. Shannon and I struggled to follow.

"Tammy!" Dad grabbed Mom and lifted her off the ground. "Thank God you're safe."

"Of course, I'm safe." Mom reached out to me to pull me close. "Did you get my text?"

I let her kiss my face. "I did."

Dad broke his embrace. "I can't tell you how relieved I was to know you were OK, but it's not the same as seeing for ourselves."

Mom kissed my face again, then she slapped it playfully. "You just left the house without telling me where you were going. I was worried sick. And when the earthquake hit and everything started falling off the shelves, I ran out of the house and tried to call you, but there was no service. Did you go to your father's office?"

I said, "I knew Dad was in trouble, so Shannon and I went to his office. The earthquake hit, and my car had been damaged, so we went on foot. By the time we got to Dad's building, it was already falling apart."

"He saved my life, Tammy," Dad interrupted. "He and Shannon pulled me from the rubble just before a giant sinkhole swallowed my entire building."

Mom went to give Shannon a hug. "Thank you, but what about your mother?"

"I got a text from her too. She's OK."

Dad bent down and whispered something in Mom's ear. I couldn't hear what he had said, but by the tears streaming from Mom's eyes, I knew what he had told her. She reached out with both arms and held me so tight, I could hardly breathe.

Through her crying, she said, "You've come back to us, Elijah?"

I looked her straight in the eyes. "Yes, Mom. I'm back."

CHAPTER 28

OUR FIRST NIGHT at Corazon Park was controlled chaos. As more and more people made their way to the sanctuary for food and shelter, soldiers continued to keep the peace and facilitate the wounded getting medical attention. The Red Cross came with supplies, and more gigantic tents went up across the park. Dylan and Brandon texted us in short bursts, since the cellular service was extremely slow. Their houses had been damaged, but not to the point where it was uninhabitable. The governor had enacted martial law, and we wouldn't be able to see them until tomorrow.

Over dinner at one of the large tents, Mom went into more detail about her ordeal. Our house, no doubt, had suffered tremendous damage, and she believed we'd have to rebuild. All of our neighbors had gathered near the entrance to our subdivision after the quake subsided. They divided themselves into small groups and went to find any survivors in the rubble, but they had come across so many of our friends who had died. With limited resources, they did the best they could. Eventually, they gathered all they could and walked the five miles to Corazon Park together.

Rows of cots underneath another large tent served as our overnight accommodations, and there were portable bathrooms all over the place. All I wanted was a hot shower, but that would have to wait. Mom smiled every time she called me Elijah. I knew she had a lot of questions, and as a family, we had much to discuss, but those things would also have to wait. It stayed warm overnight, which made it difficult to sleep, but eventually, I dozed off.

Instead of a deep red sky, the deep hues of pinks, purples, and oranges lit up the horizon. The grass was up to my chest, and a warm breeze tickled the back of my neck. It was a picture-perfect morning, and even though I knew this was a dream, I was relieved the storms and visions of the end of the world were no longer plaguing me.

Elijah.

I whirled around to find myself staring at my own image. Or at first, that's what I thought it was. The dead giveaway was the longer hair and the almost hazel eyes. Jonah's opaque image came into focus until his body looked completely solid and real.

"You did it," Jonah said with a wide grin.

I took several more steps towards him, but I didn't dare get too close. Maybe it would have been against the rules or something. "Is this just a dream?"

"What do you think?"

I replied without giving it a second thought, "It's more."

Jonah didn't confirm my assumptions, but I could tell I was right. "You have shaken off all of the illusions holding you back. It took some work, but your anger is gone."

"What now?" I asked him.

"Just as always, it is all up to you," Jonah replied.

This was too much fortune cookie crap. "An earthquake just wiped out St. Louis. It's not always up to me. I can't control whether a tornado or a 7.0 earthquake kills thousands of people. So much is out of my hands."

My brother's face hardened. "Yes, very true. That leaves you with…"

"Myself," I said. "Like you said, it's all up to me."

Jonah's image already started to fade, and I wanted to just talk with him forever. I wanted him to answer all my questions. Knowing he'd disappear soon, I threw him just one. "Are you in heaven? And don't throw my own question back at my face."

"I can't answer that." Jonah said with a frown. "What I can tell you is this: There's more."

His reply was good enough for me. I could see

through his ghostly body. "I miss you."

He looked as if he might say something, but the wind swept away his image. For just one moment, I was beyond depressed. I had lost him all over again, but if there's more beyond our lives, then I knew Jonah wasn't gone forever.

We had said goodbye, but it was only a goodbye for now.

After everyone in camp had breakfast of powdered eggs and some white bread, Dylan and Brandon found their way to our sector of the camp. Dylan's truck was left without a scratch during the earthquake, but he had to park it a good two miles away from our site. Shannon and I gave them the quick version of our story, but we promised to fill in the details once we were alone.

Brandon explained how their neighborhood was built on some ancient bedrock, so their houses were spared. Other than some expensive cosmetic stuff that would have to wait to be repaired, their homes were fortunate to have not been leveled. It would be some time before they had electricity and running water, but at least they had a roof over their heads.

They both had barely escaped their own catastrophes. Dylan pushed his mother out of the way of a falling chandelier, and Brandon saved a neighbor's life by pressing on the lady's severed femoral artery until help came. Shannon and I knew there was more to their stories, and they would share them with us at a better time and place.

My phone continued to buzz, which was weird. It had shut off last night after dinner when my battery had completely died. The Red Cross was in the process of installing cell phone charging stations powered by generators, but I hadn't had the chance to hook up my phone. When I looked at the screen, it said I had received a voicemail from an unknown caller.

I should have waited until I had left the group for some privacy, but I listened to my message on speaker mode. At first, it was just static, then Jonah's voice broke through.

"I'm proud of you, bro."

Mom lunged at my phone, with Dad right behind her. "Replay!"

I hit rewind.

"I'm proud of you, bro." The static returned, but only for a moment. "Give Mom and Dad a hug for me." And then the message ended.

Dad took my phone, took it off speaker, and listened to it again. "Is that…Jonah?"

Dylan and Brandon exchanged puzzled looks.

"I have a lot to explain," I told them before turning to Dad. "Yes. He's been coming to me in my dreams too."

Mom embraced me almost as hard as she had the night before. "I'm so sorry. You were trying to tell us this the other night. I should have believed you."

Dad listened to it again before handing me my dead phone. "No, I'm the one who completely shot you down. I'm sorry."

"It's OK. I had to work it out on my own," I said. "And I know we have a lot of work ahead of us still." I motioned towards my friends. "Is it OK if we leave the camp and have a little talk? I need to tell them everything."

Mom had her big no face on, but she wavered. "It's so dangerous out there. Debris everywhere. Weakened buildings that could collapse at any time. Maybe looters."

"It's OK, Mrs. Ashe," Dylan said. "I was able to navigate here just fine. They cleared out all the stuff on the streets. Highways are still a mess, but I know what roads are safe and clear."

She looked at Dad for confirmation before she said, "OK, but don't be gone too long. The curfew in St. Louis County is seven o'clock. Where will you go?"

I couldn't tell her where I wanted and needed to go, so I told her, "We're just going to go to Dylan's house. It's nearby, and you heard how his house is safe. We have a lot to discuss."

Brandon slapped me on the back. "You sure do. You need to explain to us why you'd leave yourself a voicemail."

It was difficult to concentrate on telling Dylan and Brandon our entire story with the dreaded devastation everywhere. Dylan had to drive slowly and carefully around the debris still littering the road, but I was amazed we were actually able to get back onto Rock Road.

When Dylan and Brandon went into greater detail about their ordeals, there was one common denominator between them. They both were prepared to act just moments before the initial massive shockwave hit. Their instincts put them on high alert, which helped them avoid the helplessness that usually follows the immediate shock during an emergency. They were both heroes.

"OK, now you have to tell us what the hell is going on," Dylan said as he maneuvered around large concrete blocks on the road.

Brandon swiveled around from the passenger's seat. "Yeah. I get the feeling we're literally missing something huge here."

I started my explanation with my final confrontation in Wells Springs with the Mothman the night the Cardinals had beat up on the Reds 14-2. I described how the creature had transformed itself into Brian K. Morris, and that I brutally attacked and killed him. That darkest moment had become a cleansing of sorts. Then I had to go back to the day Jonah had been killed and explain how and why I had assumed my dead brother's identity. Everything made sense to Brandon right away.

"I knew something wasn't right about you after Jonah died," Brandon said. "I'd been friends with you two since preschool, and something was definitely off."

Dylan asked more of the practical questions, like the death certificate with the wrong name and my school records. These were details to be dealt with later, I explained. What mattered now was I had finally dropped the illusion. I was no longer living a lie. I might not ever completely forgive Brian K. Morris for killing Jonah, but the hate fueling me had evaporated.

I told them, "I've been pretending to be Jonah for so long, it's going to be interesting to learn who I really am. I'm just relieved I didn't lose my true self after nine years of wearing Jonah's mask."

"You think you have the Mothman to thank for all of that?" Dylan asked me.

"I think so," I replied. "At the very least, it acted as the bridge between me and Jonah. It was responsible for connecting all of us to our lost loved ones, like you with your grandfather. Or Brandon with his deceased aunt." I patted Shannon on the shoulder. "And you with your father."

"Yeah." Shannon was only half-listening, as she was busy texting back and forth with her mother. "Mom hopes to meet me at Corazon Park this evening. We can't be gone for too long."

"It's only ten in the morning," I reminded her. "Besides, we'll be back at camp soon."

Dylan slowed down when my messed-up Camry came into view. My car remained untouched, but it looked pathetic all banged up and crooked on the grassy island off to the side of the road. I'm sure Dad had great insurance on his old Toyota.

We turned down the industrial road, but we couldn't get far. Concrete barricades prevented us from traveling further. News vans filled the streets, along with heavily armed soldiers guarding the area. The landfill was a about a mile from here. Dylan parked his truck along a side road, and we walked towards all of the chaos.

All we could do was stay back and listen to the reporters taping their newscasts. I didn't see any local stations here, as all of these vans had come from the big cable news channels. They talked about the contamination from the landfill, and the fear that radioactive material had seeped into the Missouri River. If such a thing had happened, it would poison the drinking water not just for St. Louis, but if the poison flowed into the Mississippi River, it could affect people from the Gateway City to the Gulf of Mexico.

"Our way is blocked. What should we do, Jonah?" Shannon let out a heavy sigh. "I'm sorry. It's going to be tough remembering to call you by your real name."

"Don't worry about it." I knew we wouldn't have to wait long. "Just sit tight for a couple minutes."

We got out of Dylan's truck, but we kept our distance from the media circus about fifty yards away. The moment I felt the air shift, as if it was suddenly charged with electricity, I turned to the sky. Shannon, Dylan, and Brandon did the same.

Shannon, with her super-vision, exclaimed, "I see it!"

Out of the distant trees, the giant creature soared above the landfill, flapping its gray wings only a few times. One by one, the cameramen pointed their equipment upwards, and all the reporters' chattering came to an abrupt halt. Everyone watched it circle three times overhead. It was high enough to keep the details of its form a mystery to the naked eye, but it soared close enough to help anyone realize they weren't watching a giant owl or vulture.

Some tribes called it the Thunderbird. The Illiniwek of the Cahokia civilization near Alton, Illinois called it the Piasa Bird. People from West

Virginia named it the Mothman. Despite whatever name we gave the winged creature that was able to travel between worlds or dimensions, to me, it would always be my guardian angel.

I mumbled a thank you to the creature before it sped westward and disappeared back up into the clouds. After another couple of minutes of silence, the four of us got back into Dylan's truck to begin the work of putting our lives back together.

But we were stronger now, thanks to the Mothman.

CHAPTER 29

Three Months Later

THANKSGIVING WAS JUST around the corner, and we would be sharing it with Mr. Ron O'Dell and his family. He and Dad did whatever they could to keep the business sort of running, but the loss of the warehouse was devastating. Mr. O'Dell vowed to rebuild.

We had been staying at their house, which was a bit weird at first, but eventually, we fell into a routine. Going to school at the mall, however, was never going to feel normal. Eleven in our class had died. Forty-three students in all lost their lives. Half of the surviving student body continued their education at the mall, and the rest of the kids moved away.

Uncle Charlie and Maverick had gotten word their rental home in Cape Girardeau had been leveled from the earthquake, since they were less than one hundred miles from the epicenter. They found a temporary place up near Chicago, but they were on their way to St. Louis for Thanksgiving. I had a lot to tell Maverick when he arrived.

Shannon and her mom stayed in town, and they were fortunate enough to stay at a co-worker's house. Brandon and Dylan were treated like kings by their neighbors. Utilities were down for a long time, and it was rough going for a while, but slowly, we adjusted to our new normal.

Our drinking water was deemed safe, for now, but more tests needed to be done. The EPA promised that the contamination had been contained. Out of the major cities in the region, Memphis and St. Louis were hit the hardest. Throughout Missouri, Tennessee, Kentucky, Illinois, Arkansas, Indiana, Alabama, and Mississippi, over eighty-thousand people were injured or killed. Over three-thousand had died. The final stats for St. Louis weren't tallied up yet.

Being able to be in the same makeshift classroom with Shannon, Dylan, and Brandon was my therapy. We never talked much about our paranormal ordeal, and that seemed to make us go backwards instead of forwards. With my tendency to relive the past with too much detail, I forced myself to stay in the moment. Nothing was more important than right now. And in my immediate future, I looked forward to celebrating Thanksgiving.

The cool thing about the O'Dell's house, other than its size, was how it sat right next to some baseball fields. No one had played on them in three months, but I liked walking around when I felt the need to be alone for a few moments. I missed having a car, but I didn't need one if I had the urge to get away.

On the evening before the official kickoff to the holidays, a bunch of kids were playing baseball at the second field. I watched them from afar, imagining Jonah out there as a seven-year-old in little league t-ball. I totally sucked at it, but he was more of a natural athlete. He could crank the ball pretty far right off the tee, and I bet he could've been good enough to make varsity on Monument High's baseball team.

A tiny girl took the underhanded pitch deep to left field, and I laughed out loud when the ball sailed right over the fielder's head. In the parking lot next to me, a black Mercedes pulled in. For a moment, I panicked. It would have been easy to cut through a neighbor's yard and get back to Mom and Dad helping the O'Dells prepare Thanksgiving dinner. Instead, I commanded my legs to take me to their car.

The driver's side opened, and Agent Stewart got out. Agent Perkins exited without his fedora. The rear door swung open, and Dr. Park stepped out and waved before he walked towards me. He looked like he might shake my hand, but he crossed his arms instead.

"I never did get that call from you," Dr. Park said.

The ringing in my ears alerted me to what he was trying to do. "Get out of my head."

Dr. Park smirked, and the sensation of his mind-invasion dissipated. "I guess I should call you by your proper name, Elijah."

"It doesn't matter what you call me." If I still had the phone he had given me, I would have thrown it at him. "Here's what I will tell you. You'll never be able to capture the Mothman. It's not a monster or a simple creature you can sedate and dissect. It's something you, me, or anyone else can never fully comprehend."

"That's a large assumption," Dr. Park said as he moved in closer to me.

My first instinct was to back away, but I didn't budge. "Level 6 trying to solve the Mothman mystery is like a dog chasing its tail. There's no point, and you'll only get tired and dizzy. Sometimes, mysteries shouldn't be solved."

I knew Dr. Park was teetering between showing me exactly what he and his secret government agents could do to me to make me talk and just walking away so he could chase whatever unknown phenomena Level 6 deemed was important enough to examine and weaponize for the sake of national security.

"Sounds like you made a new friend," Dr. Park said with a slight grin.

I shook my head. "The Mothman isn't a friend, but it's not an enemy either."

"Tell me more." Dr. Park's dark eyes narrowed.

"I will tell you only what I'm allowed to tell you." My dreams had returned to normal, but I still saw flashes of what was to come. I never shared them with anyone, however. "There is something new I can share," I said, hoping he'd take the bait.

Dr. Park considered my offer for a quick moment. "Proceed."

"The Mothman will be in California in exactly nineteen months." I let my words hang in the air for a long time. "Mount Shasta. Many will die, and the gateway which allows the Mothman to get from over there to over here will open again."

"Nineteen months." Dr. Park pulled out his little notepad and scribbled on it. "Have a wonderful holiday, Elijah." He peeled away his jacket, and I knew he was going to put a bullet through my head with his pistol. Instead, he held out a long, silver feather. "An early Christmas present." He handed it to me with a genuine smile. "And welcome back."

The Level 6 agents climbed back into their car, but I asked Dr. Park before he got in, "Can you answer just one thing for me?"

He stopped for a moment before nodding.

"Perkins and Stewart. Are they even human? They didn't know what the Gateway Arch was. Even when it's scorching outside, they're wearing their suits and not breaking a sweat. Not to mention they can charge a phone battery with their hands and their will-bending superpowers."

Both agents' faces remained as hard as stone.

Dr. Park chuckled. "They are as much human as you are Vietnamese."

"How about you, Doctor?" Had I pushed my luck with him? I waited for his eyes to go black so he could wipe my memory. "Never mind. I don't want to know."

Without saying another word, Dr. Park got into the rear seat, shut the door behind him, and the Mercedes sped away.

I stood there for several minutes before I went back to watching the kids play baseball. While staring at the children running in the dirt, I caressed the Mothman's feather with my free hand. I had given Dr. Park the last premonition I had to give, and now, all I could do was hope.

Hope for a better tomorrow.

Hope that when I look in the mirror, I will always see the real me.

Hope I never see the Mothman again for the rest of my life.

A cold gust of artic wind came from the north, and without giving it much thought, I threw the feather into the air. The breeze took it high above my head before floating into the open field where it got caught in the stiff blades of dead grass. After a moment of hesitation, I ran to the feather, picked it up, and put it in my pocket.

THE END

ACKNOWLEDGEMENTS

I grew up in St. Ann, Missouri, a small suburb near the airport. As a child, I often crossed the large creek that ran just behind our house to get to the park. If we weren't busy navigating the large stepping stones in the running water, we'd stop to have rock skipping contests. Little did we know that Coldwater Creek would bring pain and misery to so many.

The radioactive poison found at the West Lake Landfill in nearby Bridgeton and Coldwater Creek wouldn't make the news until decades later when my neighbors took notice of all the people in the region who had become sick or lost their lives to rare cancers and other illnesses.

I'd like to take the time to acknowledge and thank all the residents of Bridgeton, St. Ann, Hazelwood, and Maryland Heights who have been working tirelessly for years to get answers from the EPA, Congress, and Republic Services. You DO MAKE A DIFFERENCE.

This book took a good four years to complete, and I want to thank my family for tolerating all the hours I spend hunched over the keyboard. I love you.

Thank you to my editor and fellow tennis enthusiast Alex Neupert for shining my manuscript up and making it presentable. You are an editing ninja. I appreciate the work you put in to make *Gateway*

Mothman awesome.

Special thanks to Dominic Reyes for bringing my vision to life with your artwork. Your skills are TRUTH!

Writer's Block sucks, so thanks to my publisher, Quixotic Publishing, for giving me a swift kick in the pants. I needed a push to get creative again, and this book will finally see the light of day thanks to you.

People in the St. Louis area are still fighting the good fight in an effort to get the government to do something about the poison in the ground and water that's made so many residents sick. We want a safe and permanent solution to the contaminated sites, buyouts for residents who live close to the landfill and Coldwater Creek, and property assurance for people who live near the radioactive toxins our government illegally dumped.

You can learn more here:
http://www.stlradwastelegacy.com
http://www.coldwatercreekfacts.com

ABOUT THE AUTHOR

JAY NOEL can often be found daydreaming his life away in St. Louis where he lives with his family. With all the fantastical stff going on his brain, he writes to get it all out of his head and onto paper. Otherwise, he'd go insane. Jay marvels at how people actually want to read all this crazy stuff he creates, which brings him much joy. He especially loves meeting his readers in person at science fiction-fantasy cons throughout the Midwest. Jay has been blogging since 2005, and he gets a kick out of connecting with other bloggers and writers. If he's not busy writing and reading, you'll find him on the tennis court.

www.jaynoelbooks.com

Made in the USA
Lexington, KY
07 September 2018